Potions & Notions:
The Legacy of Rabbit Hash, Kentucky

By: Callie Clare

Potions & Notions: The Legacy of Rabbit Hash, Kentucky

Author: Callie Clare

Original cover photo courtesy of the Cincinnati Museum Center – Cincinnati Historical Society Library. Cover artwork alteration by The Merlot Group.

ISBN: 978-0-9816123-2-4

Published by:

The Merlot Group, LLC, P.O. Box 302, Covington KY 41012-0302

(859) 743-1003, www.merlotgroup.com

Acknowledgements

This book has been adapted from my MA thesis entitled An Ethnographic Look at Rabbit Hash, Kentucky written at Bowling Green State University in Bowling Green, Ohio in 2007. There I had the support and funding of the Department of Popular Culture as well as the guidance of Dr. Lucy Long, Dr. Marilyn Motz, and Dr. Montana Miller to whom I am especially thankful. Also, a great big thanks to my parents, Don and Sue Clare, for moving me to Rabbit Hash at such a young age and forcing me to accept the weird as a part of life, often times the best part. Also, if it weren't for the time and energy that they, along with the other board members and Rabbit Hash community, put in to Rabbit Hash, this wonderful town may have only existed in the past. I am especially grateful to my dad, Don, for dedicating much of his life to the preservation of the town and for sharing all of his research and photos with me. I am also very appreciative for the help, encouragement, and support of the Rabbit Hash Historical Society members who provided me this opportunity to publish this work and share it with others, with a special thanks to Shawn Masters and The Merlot Group for working with me to create the finished product. Thank you, also, to everyone who agreed to be interviewed for this project and participated in my research in any way and to everyone in the Rabbit Hash community for making this such a wonderful place to call home.

Dedication

This book is dedicated to Lowell Lee (Louie) Scott. If not for his dedication to preserving the heritage of his hometown, Rabbit Hash would not exist today.

Downtown Rabbit Hash looking upriver. (Photo taken by author)

INTRODUCTION

Wherever I go, I am always seen as the girl from Rabbit Hash, Kentucky. I don't have a problem with this. In fact, I'm actually quite proud of my hometown and enjoy telling stories of Rabbit Hash to those who have never heard of the tiny town. I explain that today, Rabbit Hash is officially only a three and a half acre plot of land along the Ohio River, just across from Rising Sun, Indiana and thirty miles downriver from Cincinnati, Ohio in rural Boone County, Kentucky. These three and a half acres are also referred to as "downtown Rabbit Hash." It used to be an official town with its own post office, but today it is unincorporated. There is only one road that passes through downtown Rabbit Hash called Lower River Road. It is one lane so when two cars happen to meet, there's a standoff until one of them pulls to the side. There is also only one stop sign in the actual town but several more if you drive around the loop, or East Bend Road (so called because of the bend in the Ohio River). Many locals refer to this drive as a trip around the Muddy (for the muddy Ohio River).

Rabbit Hash is surrounded only by the Ohio River, hills, woods, and farmland. The nearest grocery store, high school, hospital, office building, shopping district, or stop light is twenty miles away which leaves the Rabbit Hash residents somewhat secluded. While the actual in-town population of the three-and-a-half acre Rabbit Hash downtown is only one, there are a few hundred people living within the loop. But because the town is unincorporated and really has no set boundaries, measuring the population is practically impossible. Therefore, the claim of being a resident of Rabbit Hash is more of a bragging right than fact but does require some proximity to the downtown area. Being dubbed a local also depends on whether or not an individual chooses to actively participate in the Rabbit Hash community. Some individuals in the area choose to avoid the downtown area and simply live a quiet and rural life away from traffic and congestion. Others, however, are quite involved in the community and are visible in Rabbit Hash at any given time. Using this requirement of what constitutes a local therefore includes many individuals that don't live within the confines of the loop, but farther away from town.

Today, Rabbit Hash is owned by the Rabbit Hash Historical Society and consists of nine structures. Entering the town from downriver, the first of these structures is a large residential log cabin high on a hill to the right. Just down the hill from the cabin is a smaller cabin, the third oldest building in Rabbit Hash, which currently houses an archaeology firm. Across the street from these cabins is a much smaller log structure: the Rabbit Hash Historical Society museum. Next to it is the barn, the scene of many community events and the summer barn dances. Back to the right is the small blacksmith shop that now holds antiques for purchase. Above the blacksmith shop is the very long and awkward looking "Iron Works" which has served many functions over the years but is currently divided into an antique shop, a winery shop, storage, and the Hashienda (which can be rented out for a Rabbit Hash sleep-over). Past the barn and the Iron Works, the road turns to the right, away from the river. To the left is a small woodshed and immediately next to it is the Rabbit Hash General Store, the treasure and centerpiece of the small town and the heart and soul of the community. The last building in town, on the other side of the General Store, is the newest edition to town: a state-of-the-art wooden four-stall outhouse. It is a picturesque tiny American town with the community to match, but Rabbit Hash and I have a history.

My relationship with Rabbit Hash, Kentucky has been a tumultuous one with high highs and low lows. As a child living in a small apartment with my parents, my favorite thing to do was to go to Rabbit Hash. I would "help" Dad work on the log cabin he was building for our family high atop a hill overlooking the Ohio River and Rising Sun, Indiana. Before the walls were completed, we would camp in the house. During the evening, we would head down to the store and see who was around. I would get to pick out penny candies to put in my small brown paper bag and then sit on the front porch to eat it all, chewing the gum until it lost its flavor and immediately replacing it with a brand new piece. Mom and Dad would chat with other residents on the porch of the store as I chased around other children and the local dogs (or was chased by the mean chickens). It was a wonderful place to grow up.

Once in middle school, I wanted to go to the mall more and would rather spend time in the subdivisions where my friends lived than in the old General Store. At that time, Dad wanted me to participate in a county-wide children's history project: my sister and I were to write the history of Rabbit Hash for a local book. Our disinterest in the project led to Dad writing a history based on his own research of the town. He excluded all of the big words he would use otherwise and my sister and I were then given credit for "The History of Rabbit Hash" in *Ancestry: Our Ohio River Heritage*. These credits read, "By Caitlyn Clare and Callie Clare with assistance from Donald E. Clare, Jr." I still feel pangs of guilt when I see this particular book on the shelf at the General Store or my grandparents' house because I was a fraud and a cheater for letting Dad do all of the work. He attempted to convince me that I assisted in the project but I only remember providing my own bio.

In high school I was preoccupied with finding a deeper existence which I thought could only be obtained in certain hip areas of the nearby metropolis of Cincinnati, especially at punk rock clubs. Living out in the "Boonies" or "the sticks" and so far away from school, the subdivisions where my friends lived, the city, and the mall kept me secluded and unable to reach my full potential, or so I thought. Plus, my friends' parents didn't want to drive them all the way to my house which often left me feeling lonely and resentful of my tiny rural town.

In college, I moved away, but only forty-five minutes from home. After two years in the dorms, I decided living in a building with girls and hairspray was not for me so I commuted to and from my parents' log cabin in Rabbit Hash. It felt good to be back home after being away for a bit. The major turning point in my relationship with Rabbit Hash happened the summer that I turned twenty when Terrie Markesbery, who runs the General Store, offered me a job. My shift was one of the busiest; 2:30 until 7:00 on Saturday afternoons with some Sunday afternoons and all-day Friday shifts. I took her up on the offer, and through my job at the Store I fell in love with the town once again. All my desire to be in the city was gone and so was the ridicule I had experienced in high school for being a "redneck" that lived in the middle of nowhere. I put all of that behind me and grew proud of the town and the fact that I was fortunate to have grown up in Rabbit Hash. I was also very excited that on any given weekend there were so many people willing to travel from all over the tri-state area to enjoy the town for an afternoon. Perhaps the most rewarding part of my job was when I began to realize that I was surrounded by a very strong community of "locals," which I was welcomed into with open arms. They were always together, always inclusive, and always having fun. Eventually I found that I would rather stay in Rabbit Hash with the locals after my afternoon shift than drive to Florence, Newport, or Cincinnati to meet up with friends from school. The Rabbit Hash locals became my circle. And the more time I spent in the town, the more I noticed; the town is a living thing with clear patterns and a pulse of regular activity. While working in the store, from my perch at the register, I would write in my journal, describing the activity: who of the locals were around and what they were doing, the tourist and motorcycle traffic going in and out of town, and the reactions of first-time visitors when they experienced all that Rabbit Hash has to offer. It was always my hopes that I could write a book about Rabbit Hash because it was obvious to me that what happens in Rabbit Hash is special and something worth studying.

After I graduated college, I took a year off from school and worked in downtown Cincinnati. I couldn't wait until my day in the city ended and I made the long and congested trek across the Ohio River back to Rabbit Hash to unwind with the rest of the locals. One year in the real world was enough and I went back to school at Bowling Green University for my MA in Popular Culture. The freedom of that program allowed me the perfect opportunity to write about Rabbit Hash for my MA thesis. This book is adapted from that project. Because of that, it deals mostly with the history of the town, the community, and the town's appeal to both those in and outside the community. I'll be the first to admit that much more can be, and has been, written on Rabbit Hash but it is my hope that my research and analysis will answer the most frequently asked questions about the town.

I have some selfish reasons for sharing my version of the Rabbit Hash story. Rabbit Hash is famous in the Cincinnati – Northern Kentucky area for its history, its politics, its attraction for motorcycles, and its role as a venue for some of the hippest Cincinnati bands (all of which will be discussed at length later). It therefore also attracts lots of attention in the form of television, radio, film, print, and word of mouth. My pride gets in the way when someone other than me or one of the other locals is doing the talking about the town. I do, however, have reasons other than these selfish ones. There is something important about this town. Otherwise I wouldn't have to worry about the outsiders. The attraction so many people have to Rabbit Hash says something important about the town and that is what I want to concentrate on with this project. What exactly is it about Rabbit Hash, Kentucky that attracts so many people? What keeps people coming back and paying any attention to this tiny place? Why do people want to be so connected to the town?

Because of the nature of these questions, it seemed that the most logical way for me to collect information would be to go directly to members of the community and rely on their observations, as well as my own. I therefore employed ethnographic techniques such as participant observation and interviews. Because I was already a member of the Rabbit Hash community with the historical knowledge of the town and an understanding of how it operated, I was able to jump right in and start interviewing people I had known all my life and actively take notes. I feel as if my connection to the community has resulted in the gathering of very rich information and a very honest and unique look into the town and its people. Obtaining helpful informants was also quite simple for me since I did have these pre-established relationships. I picked informants that I knew would be interested in the project and could provide some interesting insight. Many were chosen because of their roles in the community, such as my father, Don Clare, who is the town historian and President of the Rabbit Hash Historical Society, Bob, who has lived in Rabbit Hash the longest, and Terrie Markesbery, the operator of the Rabbit Hash General Store. I also made sure to spend a great deal of time interviewing several of the locals who spend the most time at the General Store since these individuals represent the most active members of the Rabbit Hash community.

When researching the history of the town, I used Don Clare as my main source. He has a wealth of knowledge and obtained much of this through oral communication with members of the community who have since passed away. He is also quite familiar with all that has been written about the town and directed me to many sources, most of which he has in his possession. Therefore, some of my research was archival: looking at old photos, genealogies, local histories, flood information, ferry bonds, and official Rabbit Hash Historical Society documents.

I also used textual analysis in the study of the town when looking at the stories written about it and examining the ways in which the town is presented in news specials, television programs, and documentaries made about it. This provides an understanding of what outsiders think of the town and shows how media shapes the town to conform to a particular purpose or ideology.

My data therefore consisted of years of experience, active note taking over the course of a year, archival information, media texts, and the transcribed interviews. What I found in the data was not only the facts about the town, but also what purpose the town serves and what it means to those living in and visiting Rabbit Hash.

One of the reasons I feel Rabbit Hash is so popular and regularly draws in both locals and tourists is what Grant McCracken defines as displaced meaning[i]. In many ways, Rabbit Hash, the General Store, and the products in the store serve as bridges to the ideal, golden age of America, and encompass all of the values of that particular time. Therefore, as McCracken suggests, visitors experience the town as tangible proof of the belief that the golden age is something that we can still obtain as long as we are in the right place and consuming the right goods. It is possible for us to live a different but ideal life, if only for an afternoon, through Rabbit Hash and the goods, community, and entertainment it provides.

The look and antiquity of Rabbit Hash also brings people closer to the apparent authenticity of a particular golden age, as Jean Baudrillard theorizes[ii]. Because Rabbit Hash is an antique, it is closer to the model (the original) than it is to the series (replications), in Baudrillard's terms, thus making it seem more authentic to America's rich past. This illusion of authenticity accounts for the draw Rabbit Hash has to outsiders and the strong feelings of ownership the locals have for it.

When discussing Rabbit Hash in terms of the community, I find Victor Turner's idea of communitas to be valuable[iii]. In many ways, the community in Rabbit Hash is seen as ideal and the members of the community continue to act as if it is. Turner's theories concerning liminality are also relevant to this discussion of Rabbit Hash. Because there is very little industry in the town outside of the few successful farms, most people must travel many miles for work every day. The weekends, however, are a different story and act as a liminoid ritual, suspending the everyday and the social structures observed by the locals during the weekdays. Turner states that liminality "is often the scene and time for the emergence of a society's deepest values"[iv]. It is during the weekends that all town functions are held and community bonding is most evident, thus fortifying that connection as the deepest value in the Rabbit Hash community.

Another aspect of the Rabbit Hash community is that the locals are often performers. My folklore background has led me to recognize how performance plays a major role in the locals' lives. With the constant pressures from the outside for locals to tell their stories, members of the community are frequently thrown in front of the camera. When there is no camera around, there are often tourists. Because there is the feeling that people are constantly watching the town, many members of the community admit to "performing" or enacting certain stereotypes to conform to expectations outsiders have.

As will be exhibited throughout this book is that the appeal Rabbit Hash has to the members of its community and to outsiders is owed to a feeling of loss. Many Americans are on what could be referred to as a quest to revisit the ideals and way of life of a romanticized American past that is constantly being threatened by our contemporary society, but without permanently sacrificing our modern conveniences. Rabbit Hash serves as this bridge for many because it has proven itself to be re-adaptive in that in can be anything to anyone and has accommodated the changing times.

This project encompasses all of the topics mentioned above, moving from a discussion of the Rabbit Hash in-group to the out-group, from the private to the public. The first chapter introduces the town, its history, and how this history shapes the lives of the people living there. The first chapter was the most difficult chapter for me to write because it required that I utilize *Ancestry: Our Ohio River Heritage*, my greatest childhood shame, but also the best comprehensive recorded history of the town. The second chapter focuses on the community of Rabbit Hash and the different groups that make up the community. This community is brought together by many town functions. The biggest town function is Old Timers Day, the focus of the third chapter. This chapter emphasizes community on the private level but also the importance of Rabbit Hash to the public of the surrounding areas. The final chapter looks at the media attention Rabbit Hash receives and discusses how the locals react to the constant attention given to them from outsiders and also how the town is shaped for the public's consumption.

Overall, Rabbit Hash is evidence that people are longing for a connection to an American past. Because of its historic appearance and reputation, Rabbit Hash serves as a bridge for Americans, no matter where they live, to the imagined utopian past and all of the values that we collectively associate with the golden age of America: the small town, the tight-knit community, and the simple life.

---

[i] McCracken, Grant, "The Evocative Power of Things: Consumer Goods and the Preservation of Hopes and Ideals," in *Culture and Consumption: New Approaches to the Symbolic Character of Consumer Goods and Activities* (Bloomington: Indiana University Press, 1988), 104-117.

ii Baudrillard, Jean, *The System of Objects*, trans. James Benedict (New York: Verso, 2005).

iii Turner, Victor, *The Anthropology of Performance* (New York: PAJ Publications, 1987).

iv Ibid., 102.

CHAPTER I:
REMEMBERING LOCAL HISTORY AND RECREATING AN AMERICAN PAST

Rabbit Hash is old. It isn't the oldest place this fine country has

to offer, but for most of us, it will do. Not only is it old but it also looks

old, smells old, and feels old. Anyone can get a sense of its age just by

walking through the Rabbit Hash General Store. The hardwood floors are

worn from years of foot traffic grinding in the sandy dirt from the

surrounding riverbank and farmland. The wooden counters have been

smoothed by years of sliding merchandise, hands, and money exchange.

Everything creaks or rattles with each footstep or door closure. Hanging

from the ceiling and on the highest shelves are antiques. Some of them

are easy to name but others are so foreign, belonging to a different time

entirely. The air smells like wood smoke, river air, old wood, and dirt

disguised under a veil of incense. Usually there are several people huddled

around the wood stove in the back of the store discussing the weather,

work, or town gossip.

Rabbit Hash's history and the way it draws you into the past is

one of the town's most celebrated aspects. Everyone wants to know when

the store was built, how the town got its name, and who ran the store and

when. While much of this is documented, and those documents have

been collected by the Rabbit Hash Historical Society, other parts of the

The interior of the Rabbit Hash General Store from the entrance. (Photo taken by author)

Robert (Bob) Hayden Wilson leaning on his uncle's headstone in the Wilson Family Cemetery in Rabbit Hash. (Courtesy of the Rabbit Hash Historical Society)

history of the town have been passed on as oral histories and tales by the old timers. Luckily for Rabbit Hash, it has always had interested residents who collect as much as the information about the old times as they can, one of these individuals being my father, Don Clare. I have been fortunate enough to know many of the older residents of Rabbit Hash myself and hear the tales of the town – some of the tales have been passed down to me through Don who learned quite a bit from Robert (Bob) Hayden Wilson before his death. Bob Wilson was the grandson of James A. Wilson (first proprietor of the General Store). His legacy, along with that of hundreds of years' worth of Rabbit Hash residents, lives on in these tales and in the history of the town. Of course, stories change and new interpretations are formed every time a story is retold. It therefore becomes more and more difficult to separate facts from emotional fantasy. But how we interpret the past can tell us a great deal about today.

Besides a desire to know the history of the town, many of the members of the Rabbit Hash community appear to want to simulate the past, or at least incorporate traditional American ways of life into their modern existences. This chapter recounts a brief history of the town and explores the ways in which this history has infiltrated the lives of the Rabbit Hash community.[1]

Postcard of a Snag Boat docked at Rising Sun, IN c. 1907. (Photo courtesy of Don Clare)

Wilson family portrait featuring James A., his wife, and some of their children taken at the Wilson homestead in Rabbit Hash. James A. is seated in the front row, second from the right. (Courtesy of the Rabbit Hash Historical Society; Donated by Phyllis J. Jones)

From Carlton to Rabbit Hash

The town of Rabbit Hash, Kentucky developed and grew with Rising Sun, Indiana, directly across the Ohio River. Rising Sun, founded in 1814, was an early stopping point for steamboats traveling up and down the Ohio River because the main channel was on the Indiana side. This newly established mode of commerce allowed residents of the area to import and export goods and farm produce. So that those on the Kentucky side of the river could benefit as well, a ferry boat was established in 1813 by Edward Meeks. The boat was actually docked about two miles upriver from present-day Rabbit Hash, at Middle Creek, and this spot is referred to as Meeks Landing on older maps and in stories. With the transportation of more and more goods across the river, the need arose on the Kentucky side for a building in which to store the goods. In 1831, the Grange, an agricultural association of local farmers, built a storage building that served as a co-op repository. This building is still standing today, but is better known as the Rabbit Hash General Store, or simply the Store. When facing the store the original structure is the central timber frame bay. The two sheds on either side of it were added later. The locals would store their crops and goods in the store and it operated on a barter system. Eventually, it was transformed into a general store, operated by one proprietor, James A. Wilson, a Virginia native who moved to the area with his family at the age of ten.[2]

The earliest photo of the General Store, then called Wilson and Riddell, taken in 1894.
(Photo by Reuben Gold Thwaites; Courtesy of the State Historical Society of Wisconsin)

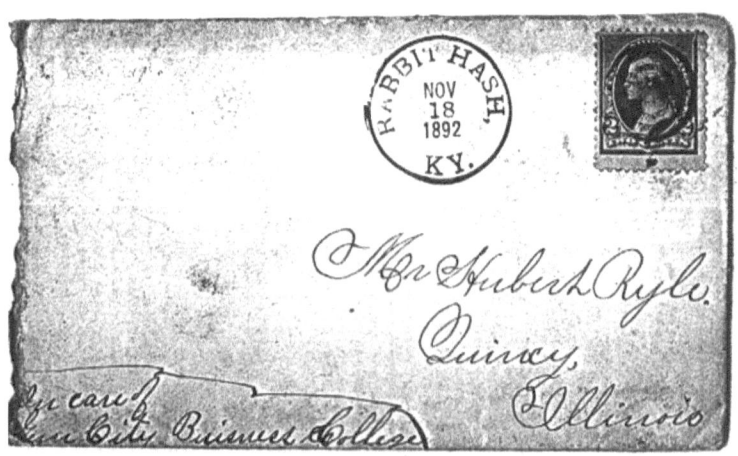

Copy of the Rabbit Hash postmark, dated 1892.
(Photo courtesy of the Rabbit Hash Historical Society)

Besides asking how old the General Store is, visitors also want to know how Rabbit Hash received such a strange name. This story is one that locals explain over and over again every time a tourist asks or a news camera comes to town. It has also been a brief topic in many local history books as well as in novelty books such as *Reaching Climax: And Other Towns Along the American Highway*. No two accounts of this story are the same, though.

To begin this long and complex history of the town's name, it is important to know that Rabbit Hash was first called Carlton after a family living in the area. Just down river from Carlton is Carrollton, Kentucky and, as Don Clare explained, the mail from the two towns was getting mixed up. Therefore, the postal service requested that those living in Carlton change the name of the town to prevent further confusion. The residents chose Rabbit Hash as the name of the town.

But why Rabbit Hash of all names? This is the most interesting, most documented, and most argued point in Rabbit Hash's history. While all documented versions of the story are very different, they all have two things in common: they all reference a dish called rabbit hash and most of them are dependent on a flood.

This first version of the tale was recorded in Professor A.M. Yealey's book, *History of Boone County Kentucky*. He claims that the name came from salt traders at a tavern at Meeks Landing and cites his sources as "old Kentucky history books, old papers, private diaries of men who explored the river front of Boone County."[3] This story is recounted in Robert Rennick's book *From Red Hot to Monkey's Eyebrow* and also claims that Rabbit Hash got its name from travelers:

> Two travelers met at the Ohio River town of Rising Sun. One was going to cross there into Kentucky and, having learned that the other had just come off the ferry, asked about the accommodations at Meek's Landing. "They're all right," said the other, "if you like rabbit hash. There's plenty of that at Meek's table."
>
> The river had been at high tide for many days, and only the day before the water level had begun to recede. Thousands of rabbits had been driven to the hillsides by high water, and Meek set his men to hunting them down to replenish his pantry.
>
> As the traveler indeed discovered when he crossed the river and boarded at Meek's tavern, rabbit hash was the order of the day – and of the week, and the month. It was so plentiful, in fact, that after a year Meek's guests were still being served healthy helpings of rabbit hash – for breakfast, dinner, and supper. It was used for midnight snacks, as appetizers, even as feed for the live-

stock, and in picnic baskets for lovers.

Rabbit hash – people got plain sick and tired of it. It seemed it just couldn't be used up. Travelers were asked to take some with them when they continued on their trips. Many an empty stomach was filled when ample portions of rabbit hash arrived at distant places courtesy of the generous humanitarians at Meek's Landing. This Boone County town on the Ohio River is still called *Rabbit Hash*.[4]

According to Don Clare, these accounts cannot be confirmed because there has never been written documentation of a tavern operating in Rabbit Hash.

The story of the name was also misreported in *Now and Then*, written by four authors from different parts of Kentucky attempting to answer a series of questions, beginning with biblical concerns. Eventually the book turns to more specific Kentucky questions about particular counties, parks, highways, and sites in the state. A section on Boone County, the county in which Rabbit Hash is located, discusses Mary Draper Ingles and how it was believed that she spent time in the area during her captivity.[5] This book credits her with the name Rabbit Hash.

At Carlton the Indians found rabbits plentiful on some small islands and the surrounding undergrowth. The

The old post office boxes in the back of the Rabbit Hash General Store. Today they serve as shelves for general merchandise such as toiletries and batteries. (Photo taken by author)

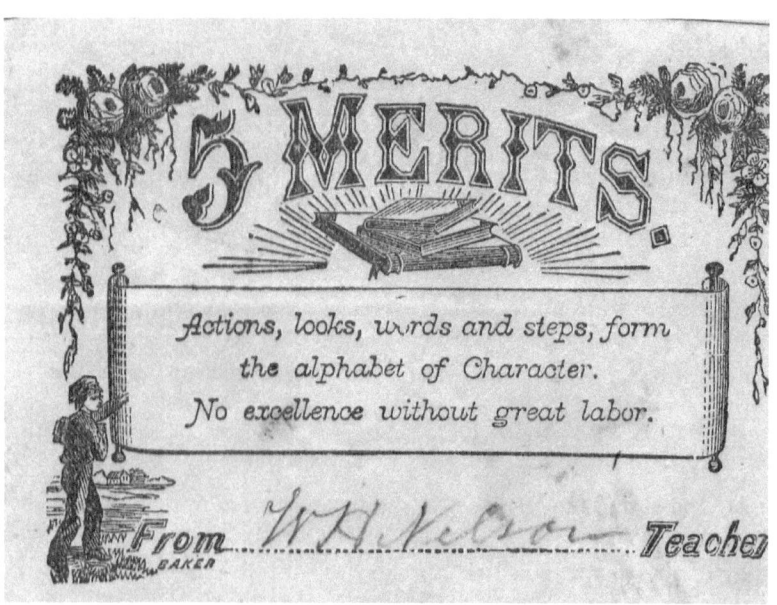

Merits signed and given by William H. Nelson to students. (Photo courtesy of Don Clare)

Indians killed many rabbits, and Mrs. Inglis being a good cook made what she called rabbit hash with the rabbit meat. Old timers have said that is the way Rabbit Hash received its name from Mrs. Inglis' rabbit hash. The party stayed at Rabbit Hash several days in August 1755.[6]

The validity of this account has been seriously questioned because of the dates. This story takes place practically seventy years before the General Store (the first building in the town) was built and some twenty years before Daniel Boone (credited with the settlement of Kentucky) even entered the state.

The story of Rabbit Hash that an inquirer will most likely hear today is the version that I have been raised to believe as the truth, most likely because my father is the greatest promoter of the tale. This story was recorded and embellished by William H. Nelson, the editor and publisher of a newspaper across the river from Rabbit Hash and a Boone County school teacher who lived in Rabbit Hash after marrying a Carlton woman. The story originally appeared in the newspaper, *The Lawrenceburgh Register*, but was also included at the end of a story he wrote entitled *The Buried Treasure: A Rabbit Hash Mystery*. No official date exists for this publication but it can be assumed that it was written around 1849 while Nelson was with *The Lawrenceburgh Register*.

How, you ask, did the name originate? It has been wisely

said that in every great emergency a genius will rise competent to guide the helm of State. As with nations, so with municipalities; and our city was not an exception to the rule.... The time when this auspicious event occurred was Christmas day. A.D. 1847. As all of your older readers know, this was during the great forty-seven flood. For several days the river had been rising steadily, until now all the houses on the bank were flooded, and the owners were compelled to seek quarters with their more fortunate neighbors.... Christmas day fell on the inauspicious season. Instead of the usual rejoicing at its advent, a pall of gloom overspread the community. No roast turkey and mince pies; no eggnog nor rum flip were to be had or expected. Instead of the usual hilarity the masculine portion of the community stood around in sheltered places and watched the great flood sweeping by in majestic grandeur, bearing on its turbulent breast a great wealth of miscellaneous drift.... Conversation was spiritless, and few words were uttered, save about some scene or incident connected with the watery panorama before them. At length one of the crowd, stimulated by hunger and visions of many past savory Christmas dinners, turned the talk to this interesting theme. Then, in turn, each one joined in by telling what he wished for or hoped to have on his festive board. One said he would have roast goose, caught in the drift the day before; another had a fat hen, caught in a similar manner; another a fat 'possum, unwarily caught napping and grinning in a hollow log; and so they went on from hog to hominy, until all but one of the party had announced their bill or fare. This one was the jester, although the butt of the company. He stood somewhat apart, shivering violently, not so much from the effects of the cold, however, as from the chronic influence on his system of over-indulgence in any and every kind of alcoholic stimulant that he could buy, beg or borrow. When it was noticed that he had taken no part in the gastronomical conversation someone asked:

"Well, Frank, what are you going to have for your Christmas dinner?"

With a leer and a wink that seemed to intensify his fit of shivering, his teeth chattering like castanets, he answered in just two words, "Rabbit Hash!"[7]

As the story goes, the locals referred to Frank as "Rabbit Hash" and over time that moniker became associated with the town.

In the film *Rabbit Hash: The Center of the Universe* (to be discussed at length in the fourth chapter), Don tells this story as the true story to how Rabbit Hash got its name. Because of the local popularity of the film and the republication of *The Buried Treasure: A Rabbit Hash Mystery* in 1997, this is the most widely known and accepted version of the tale. It is interesting to note that this version which is most accepted by the Rabbit Hash locals is also the only tale that credits the locals with the naming of the town. The other tales give credit to outside travelers or well-known heroines. In a way, promoting the tale featuring the locals leaves the Rabbit Hash residents of today entitlement to the town rather than to those just passing through. It is just one of the ways that the residents connect to the rich history of the town.

A River's Rage

As demonstrated in the tales above, Rabbit Hash and the Ohio River have quite a tumultuous relationship and the Ohio River's tendency to flow out of its banks has played a major role in shaping the town and its history. Floods tend to occur in the early part of the year with melting snow and heavy rains causing the river waters to rise. Most of the time, especially with modern dams along the river, the rising waters are not a threat and only flood the riverbanks. However, it is not uncommon to have floodwaters cover portions of Lower River Road, the one-lane road running through Rabbit Hash. At times, however, the flood waters are much more dangerous and can cover portions of the road with several feet of water, enter into, and sometimes destroy, homes and other buildings, endanger or even kill livestock, and take docks, boats, and other objects down river, never to be returned.

Floods have also repeatedly changed the face of the town. When the General Store was built, there were several other buildings in the small town including a creamery, a tobacco warehouse, and numerous homes. Unfortunately, most of these buildings were eventually lost to floods, making the General Store the oldest standing building today.

The Rabbit Hash General Store is also one of the first buildings to go under water in high flood waters, and it has been invaded several times, the first time being in 1847. Don often mentions the river legend about how the Ohio River will always return to claim and take what it had left behind the time before. And the mighty Ohio has tried to come back for the General Store but the ingenuity of the residents has prevented that. They installed a system of hooks under the store. Planted deep into the ground under the store are long metal rods with hooked ends. These are holding onto the hooked ends of rods coming from the underside of the floor of the store. When the river and creek waters rise under the store and get so high that the store starts to float, the hooks lock together

Hooks under the General Store that prevent it from floating away during high flood waters. (Photo taken by author)

On the far left side of the Iron Works building is a series of wooden plaques that serve as flood markers demonstrating how high flood waters actually were during the town's most devastating and significant floods. (Photo taken by author)

and secure the store in its present location, preventing it from floating away. Because this system has proven itself again and again with the store, similar systems have been installed on some of the newer buildings in town.

A constant reminder of the floods exists in the form of flood markers on the left corner of the iron works building. At the very bottom of the building is a piece of carved wood with the numbers "1997 64'5"." Approximately six feet up is another marker that reads "1913 1933 69'6"" and then another right above it "1884 71'1"." Still higher reads "1773 76'." Finally, at the very top of the two-story building, right under the roof, is a board carved "Flood Marker." Immediately below it is another that reads "1937 79'99"." These engravings tell the year and official number of feet at which the river crested. At Cincinnati, forty feet is considered a warning stage for a flood and flood stage is at fifty-two feet. Sixty feet is when river water enters the General Store. Having these markers visibly displayed on the side of the one of the buildings in town allows viewers to visualize what was underwater and the power and threat of the Ohio River, serving as a reminder of the town's long and turbulent history.

The most significant flood that changed the shape of the town was the 1937 flood. According to Don, the water was so high that it was over the roof of the General Store and, to this day, there is still mud in the

Rising flood waters in 1937. The buildings located in the background were all lost during the flood. (Photo courtesy of the Rabbit Hash Historical Society; Donated by Louie Scott)

The old blacksmith shop, which now carries antiques, is built on the foundation of a store moved by the 1937 flood. Note the gas pumps donated by Louie Scott which mimic those that were there before the flood. (Photo taken by author)

attic from the flood waters. This dangerous flood is also responsible for taking many of the buildings in the town including some homes, the creamery, and the tobacco warehouse. The building that is today referred to as the blacksmith shop, but houses antiques for sale, is constructed on the foundation of a building moved by the flood waters. However, this particular building, which was operated by the Ryle Brothers and sold gasoline and hardware and was referred to as the oil station, was not actually lost to the river, just moved. According to Bob, the oldest member of the Rabbit Hash community (having spent all his life, since 1928, in Rabbit Hash), several other locals, and photographic evidence, the building floated up the hill behind it and the Ryle Brothers (who also operated a second general store on that hill across from the present Rabbit Hash General Store) attached it to their other store, resulting in a very long building. This strange-looking building is still in Rabbit Hash today, located across the street from the General Store and is referred to as the Iron Works because that is where the Rabbit Hash wood-burning stoves were made in the 1970's and 1980's.

Other than the recollections Bob has of the 1937 flood, there are two other floods that stand out in the town's memory that have seriously impacted the current Rabbit Hash community. The first of these, in 1964, is not labeled on the Iron Works but crested at 66.2 feet, well below the 1937 flood. Carleen Stephens, a lifelong resident of the town and member

The Ryle Brothers' oil station (with gas pumps) across from the General Store that was moved by the flood of 1937.
(Photo courtesy of the Rabbit Hash Historical Society; Donated by Louie Scott)

Bob sits around the stove in the General Store passing out words of wisdom. (Photo by author)

of the Rabbit Hash Historical Society, was a freshman in high school in 1964 and remembers the night the river was coming up and water was getting into the store:

> It just so happened that night Cliff Stephens's [who ran the store at that time] brother had passed away and the visitation at the funeral home was that night and everybody in the community went to the funeral home of course, and we come back and the river was coming up and everybody came to the store and moved it out. I left the store at six o'clock in the morning as they brought the cash register out in a boat. And had to go home and get a bath and get ready to go to school, had not been to bed all night. And at that time they had a cooler back here and they had fresh lunch meat in it. We kept the slicer going and made sandwiches for everybody all night long…but everybody in the community was here and there was trucks that come down from Burlington to load the groceries up. They took it all down to the Methodist church and stored it.

The next major flood was in 1997. In March of that year was the last time that flood waters entered into the General Store. I, like Carleen in 1964, was a freshman in high school during that time and had been

The 1964 flood. Photo taken from the Iron Works yard.
(Courtesy of the Rabbit Hash Historical Society; Donated by the Stephens family)

The Rabbit Hash General Store in the flood of 1997. (Courtesy of the Clare family)

home from school with the flu when the waters started to rise. Although I was sick, and couldn't help, the community did come together once again and emptied the contents of the General Store and the craft shop that was located in the barn at that time, and moved them to higher ground. Because of the high waters over the road on either side of our driveway, I missed another week of school. With the use of boats and hiking, many people were able to carry on with their daily routines. While no homes or buildings were lost, many docks and boats were. As soon as the flood water receded, I found many treasures left behind by the floodwaters. I specifically remember a dead cow tangled in the brush between my home and downtown Rabbit Hash that we would all rush to one side of the school bus to glimpse as we drove past.

Rabbit Hash Reborn

While floods have been a danger to Rabbit Hash, so has modernization. Today, Rabbit Hash still appears to be an idyllic American community with the General Store at its heart. However, this was almost not the case. By the 1970's, Rabbit Hash was no longer the center of the residents' world. Many people stopped farming and started working closer to larger towns. They began shopping in the towns of Burlington, Union, and Florence and had no need to visit the tiny General Store which didn't have as much variety. By this time, there was also no ferry boat to Rising

The General Store in the 1933 flood. Note the water in 1933, 1964, and 1997 came within a few feet of one another on the General Store. (Courtesy of the Rabbit Hash Historical Society)

After the 1937 flood, this building was moved from its foundation higher up on the hill. (Photo courtesy of the Rabbit Hash Historical Society; Donated by Louie Scott)

The barn (at the time of the Kentucky Huckster craft shop) in the 1997 flood. Note the "Firestone" sign that acts as an unofficial measurement of the flood waters. (Photo courtesy of the Clare family)

The Mildred, the last ferry boat between Rabbit Hash, KY and Rising Sun, IN. The Mildred operated until 1945 when it was destroyed by ice. (Photo courtesy of the Rabbit Hash Historical Society)

An early Rabbit Hash Historical Society meeting c. 1980. Don Clare and Louie Scott on the front porch of the Rabbit Hash General Store. (Photo courtesy of the Clare family)

The front of the Iron Works building, the first building Louie Scott bought. This end currently houses a wine shop. (Photo taken by author)

Sun; what was once a strong bond between the two towns was gone and now the quickest way to Rising Sun takes over an hour by car. This left Rabbit Hash more isolated and caused many people to move away from the small river town and closer to the larger towns and cities.

Louie Scott, born and raised in Rabbit Hash, noticed what was happening and began buying up the land and buildings of Rabbit Hash (at that time, there were only three) before they were completely forgotten and torn down. The first building he purchased was the Ryle Brother's feed and hardware store which is now referred to as the Iron Works. The Iron Works is the third oldest building in Rabbit Hash and is said to have been built between 1910 and 1920. In its ninety-plus years, it has been home to a second general store, a hardware store, a pool hall (where one could also purchase some illegal whiskey), an early Ford dealership, a slaughterhouse, a storage facility, an iron works where wood burning stoves were made, an antique store, a craft shop, an office, an apartment, a wine store, and a bed-and-breakfast.

The General Store maintained a successful business over the years through proprietors such as James A. Wilson, Cal Riddell, Charles (C.W.) Craig, and his son Sheenie but the business could not survive if there was no one around to support it. Upon witnessing the young and enthusiastic Louie Scott taking an interest in the geriatric town, Cliff and Lib Stephens (son-in-law and daughter of C.W. Craig), who owned the

The other end of the Iron Works, home to the Hashienda which can be rented out for an overnight stay in Rabbit Hash. (Photo taken by author)

Cal Riddell, proprietor of the General Store in Rabbit Hash in the 1890's, on the porch of the General Store. (Photo courtesy of the Rabbit Hash Historical Society)

General Store at the time, approached Louie and asked him if he would also like to buy their store. According to Don, he took them up on their offer and sort of moved himself into the General Store, sleeping on a roll-away bed by the stove while finishing up his large log cabin on the hill in Rabbit Hash where he still lives today. Don spent quite a bit of time with Louie in Rabbit Hash watching the river go by and talking about what Louie had planned for the town. Others, such as old timer Bill Feldhaus, reveled at how Louie had taken the town, "without firing a single shot."

After Louie purchased the two stores, he purchased the second oldest building in town, the small cabin. This cabin was built in the late 1800's and had served as a doctor's office until the 1930's.[8] But when Louie purchased the building, a man referred to as Stumpy was living there. Because of the age of the building and also because of Stumpy's dirtier habits, the building was renovated and an addition was built onto it. Although Louie was not aware of the tenets of historic preservation, his goal with the restoration of the cabin was to maintain the façade of the building and expand back. Therefore, anyone who had lived in the area a hundred years ago could return, see the building, and recognize it, a major goal of historic preservation.

After the purchase of each building, there was quite a bit of work to be done. Each building was in need of stabilization and all of the old artifacts remaining in the buildings needed to be dealt with and organized.

Cliff Stephens, past proprietor of the General Store, behind the counter in the General Store. (Courtesy of the Rabbit Hash Historical Society)

Louie Scott's log cabin on the hill in Rabbit Hash. From its porch, he can still keep an eye on what is going on in town. (Photo taken by author)

Don recounts his days with Louie while cleaning out the buildings:

> So Louie got a big dumpster. I came down one night and he was just flinging stuff in the dumpster out of that building. I said, "Louie, you can't throw that stuff away. That's historic." He said, "All right, Clare. You're in charge of historic and I'm in charge of cleaning this building out," so he'd throw stuff in and I'd pull it out and put it in my truck and that's how the Rabbit Hash Historical Society started. I was in charge…. Same thing happened at the General Store. He started throwing stuff out and I'd take it out of the dumpster and keep it."

Don then took the things he had salvaged from the dumpster and created a small museum, consisting of one display case, in the back room of the General Store. The other items he saved are still lining the top shelves of the store or hanging from the ceiling. Many other items have also been stored in the barn and Iron Works or on display in the current Rabbit Hash Historical Society Museum.

Once the buildings were cleared out, their usages changed. The doctor's office was made into a more livable home and has been called home by several Rabbit Hash locals. Instead of housing locals today, it is home to an archaeology firm. In the 1970's, the building housing the feed store was transformed into an actual functioning iron works where the

The old doctor's office in Rabbit Hash taken through a car window in 1954. (Courtesy of the Rabbit Hash Historical Society; Cincinnati Pictorial Enquirer)

Antique bottles and other items found in the old Rabbit Hash buildings are on display on the top shelves of the General Store, some even hang from the ceiling. (Photo taken by author)

Rabbit Hash wood burning stoves were made. Don talks of the 1970's trend of making or getting the best wood burning stove, a phenomenon even featured in *Mother Earth News*. Don explains that the winters of 1977 and 1978 were very severe and Louie decided to make stoves to sell to the locals at an inexpensive price so that they could stay warm all winter. However, for insurance purposes, Louie would have to go through the Underwriters Laboratories (the UL) safety organization in order to sell the stoves. That process would add $250 to the price of the stoves, thus defeating the original purpose. Louie ended up giving the stoves away to the locals and then stopped making any more. Today, the stoves are present in all of the Rabbit Hash buildings and several homes in the area. They have also become collectible items often commanding prices that triple their original price.

The barn standing in Rabbit Hash was not one of the original buildings, but was built in the early 1980's. It was actually standing a few miles up the road, torn down, moved, and rebuilt near the river in downtown Rabbit Hash. While the barn was used for storage and as a place to manufacture the bank equipment that Louie designed, it was also used for barn dances and other social activities as well as a craft shop called the Kentucky Huckster featuring only Kentucky-made crafts. Since the closing of the Huckster, the barn has been divided into a roofing business's office, an art gallery, and the largest portion is still reserved for

*The Rabbit Hash Historical Society museum located in downtown Rabbit Hash.
(Photo taken by author)*

*The small cabin in Rabbit Hash, now home to an archeology firm, is the second oldest building
in town and was originally a doctor's office. (Photo taken by author)*

social gatherings and can be rented out for parties and events.

The nature of the Rabbit Hash General Store changed during the 1970's and 1980's as well. Don gives credit to the operator of the business at that time, Patty Purnell. Patty is an artist and added the old hippie element to the store. While people no longer depended on the General Store for groceries, they did depend on it as a place to socialize. Therefore much of the profit was made with the sale of beer and snacks. Rabbit Hash was also a popular lunch spot, selling lunch meat sandwiches, for men working at the East Bend Power Station which was being built just a few miles down the road in the early 1980's. Patty also began designing the first Rabbit Hash t-shirts which featured Herb, the iconic Rabbit Hash hillbilly. Herb is pictured with a long beard and lounging in tattered clothes, bare feet, and a large hat while holding a rifle on his shoulder. Since he is intended to represent the stereotypical hillbilly, his jug of homemade corn liquor is nearby. Listed under Herb are the four main products sold in the Rabbit Hash General Store and what the sign on top of the store advertises: Tobacco, Sundries, Potions, Notions. Patty credits the success of the General Store during her years of operation to the t-shirts. Enough were sold for her to use the money to keep the store stocked with all of the other products she sold. Herb is still featured on souvenirs sold in the store and he even writes guest columns in several Northern Kentucky papers and magazines as well as the Rabbit Hash

The barn in Rabbit Hash where many community events take place. (Photo taken by author)

Patty Purnell, past proprietor of the General Store, during the very first Old Timers Day on July 5, 1980. (Photo courtesy of the Clare family)

Historical Society's Website. Don Clare "dictates" Herb's words and is responsible for submitting the articles.

Although there have been some changes in Rabbit Hash since the late 1970's and early 1980's, it is this era and this particular generation of Rabbit Hash residents that shaped Rabbit Hash into the community that it is today by both drawing the locals back into town as well as appealing to visitors who were looking for a way to connect with the past. These are the individuals who found something special in Rabbit Hash and actively pursued ways to ensure the safety and preservation of the historic town.

The Rabbit Hash General Store has been designated as a Kentucky Landmark since the 1970's. However, it was the Boone County Preservation Review Board, on which Don Clare has had a seat for decades, that put the General Store and other historic structures and sites in the area on the National Register. In 1966, the National Historic Preservation Act was passed to make this register of America's historic structures and sites and it is kept by the Department of the Interior of the United States Government. Because the Boone County Preservation Review Board is a Certified Local Government it is eligible for federal money in the forms of grants. One of the most popular uses for this grant money is to fund the research and documentation required to put local buildings on this register. The General Store, along with some of the homes outside of the property of Rabbit Hash and the East Bend

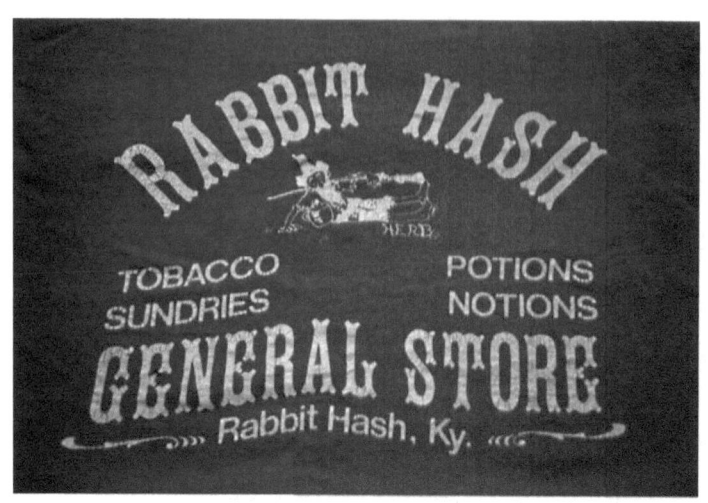

The first Rabbit Hash General Store t-shirt design featuring Herb the Hillbilly.
(Design by Patty Purnell; Photo taken by author)

The National Register Plaque located across from the Rabbit Hash General Store.
(Photo taken by author)

Methodist Church, also owned by the Rabbit Hash Historical Society, were added to the National Register based on research conducted with funds given to the Boone County Preservation Review Board.

After this successful endeavor, Don took it upon himself to attempt to get the entire town on the register as a historic district. This required a great deal of time and research. After decades of work and several failed attempts, a hired consultant finally succeeded in getting the proposal passed, and Rabbit Hash was finally added to the National Register as a historic district.

Besides being on the National Register, Rabbit Hash is also a Preserve America Community. Preserve America is an incentive on the part of former First Lady, Laura Bush, to aid in the preservation of historic towns in the United States. Both Preserve America and the National Register are more for national recognition and pride than anything else. A benefit of the Preserve America designation is the opportunity for certain grants. The National Register has more circumstantial benefits. Once on the National Register, the buildings are not guaranteed to remain on it indefinitely. Don emphasizes that "the idea of a National Register building is if the person who built it or was around then were to come back now and look at the building, he'd recognize it." Therefore, if something on the exterior of the building is altered too much, the building will be removed from the register.

*The sign marking the boundary of the Rabbit Hash National Register District.
(Photo taken by author)*

*The sign marking the end boundary of the Rabbit Hash National Register District.
(Photo taken by author)*

Although the National Register cannot save a building from being torn down by private individuals, it does guarantee that no federal funds can be used to impact it in a negative way. Before the town was even approved to be a National Register District, it was considered National Register Eligible because a nomination had been submitted. This gave Rabbit Hash the same rights as it would have if it were on the Register. This was helpful to the community in the 1990's when the Grand Victoria riverboat casino was put in at Rising Sun, Indiana, directly across the river from Rabbit Hash. Don claims that the original plan was for a bright pink boat with neon lights accompanied by a lighthouse and an amphitheatre pointing in the direction of Rabbit Hash. Because it is on the river, everything must go through the Army Corps of Engineers, which is operated with federal money, and that gave Rabbit Hash some bargaining input when it came to the final decisions on designs. The Grand Victoria turned out to look like a traditional riverboat rather than Vegas monstrosity. While Rising Sun did get approved for the amphitheatre, the lighthouse was denied because there has never been a lighthouse on the Ohio River and could be considered a threat to the historic integrity of Rabbit Hash.

Around that same time the Grand Victoria was being planned, Louie Scott decided to put the entire town of Rabbit Hash up for sale in 1992 at the price of $639,500.84. Don Clare was in charge of the sale

Preserve America sign located in front of the Iron Works, across the street from the General Store. (Photo taken by author)

The Grand Victoria Casino located across the river from Rabbit Hash in Rising Sun, Indiana. (Photo taken by author)

(called Project: Rabbit Hash) and placed an ad in *Historic Preservation News*. He accepted inquiries and sent information to interested parties. His main task was to approve any possible buyer. Anyone considered for the purchase must be someone who would continue the town's protection and preservation. The fact that an entire town was put up for sale drew quite a bit of attention but failed to conjure any serious bidders. Don and Louie became nervous with the promise of the gambling boat across the river so the town was taken off the market. Louie considered handing the town over to the Rabbit Hash Historical Society (RHHS) but that would cost both parties too much money in taxes. The RHHS couldn't afford to buy the town since it had no way of making any money and still consisted of just Louie, Don, and Sue Clare (Don's wife and RHHS secretary).

While at work one day in 2001, Don received a phone call from the lawyer of Edna Flower, a Rabbit Hash local. She informed Don that Edna had recently passed and had left something for the RHHS in her will. No one had expected that something to be the gift of $250,000. After this windfall, the RHHS invited new board members to join, Louie stepped down, and a deal was made for the purchase of the town. The Rabbit Hash Historical Society became the official owners of Rabbit Hash on December 13, 2002.

The Historical Society was incorporated in 1984 with the primary goal to maintain the historic town through spreading information about

Edna Flower as a child. Because of her generous donation, Rabbit Hash will continue to be preserved. (Courtesy of the Rabbit Hash Historical Society)

IN MEMORY AND APPRECIATION OF
EDNA B. FLOWER
FOR HER
EXTRAORDINARY GENEROSITY AND SUPPORT
TOWARD THE PRESERVATION OF THE
TOWN OF RABBIT HASH, KENTUCKY
JANUARY 2002

Plaque on the door of the museum in Rabbit Hash to commemorate Edna Flower's generous donation. (Photo taken by author)

the town, procuring and preserving artifacts relating to the history of the town and region, and preserving the buildings. This requires that it provide protection against the forces of evil that prey upon the historic town: floods, ice, fire, wind, and termites. The funding for this expensive upkeep comes from a variety of sources including donations, fundraisers, RHHS souvenir sales, tourism, and rental property. It also means making decisions that will both maintain the historic integrity and fabric of the town while accommodating as many people and town functions as possible. However, the RHHS board must abide by many government laws and guidelines, especially with the town's growing popularity. This means that the board has had to make some unpopular but necessary changes in the town in order to comply with laws and therefore ensure the continued use of the town by community members and visitors alike.

The Rabbit Hash State of Mind

Living in a National Register historic district is something that the locals are used to. There is a sense of the history that pulsates through the community and there is no denying the old buildings, the lack of running water, and the outdoor toilets. However, when asked about how they contribute to this historic location, the locals fail to see how they themselves add to the history and ambiance of the town. Most of the homes in the Rabbit Hash area are old homes and antiques are the most common decoration. Old family photos, childhood toys, family heirlooms, antique furniture, and trinkets found in places like old barns are common in many of these homes. Many people, like Duane Doyle and Don Clare, admit to collecting "old" things. Duane is known in the area for being an extremely helpful community member. He served on the RHHS and is often seen around town mowing grass, taking out the trash, helping to stock coolers, or playing with the children. He is also known to be somewhat of a scavenger, in the nicest sense of the term, in that he is more than willing to tear down any old building that is no longer wanted. He takes it apart and keeps all of the materials and finds some amazing antiques in the process. Like Don did at the conception of the RHHS, Duane keeps all of these old things because they are a piece of history. He also loves the way old rusty tools look and how they constantly remind him of how work was much harder in the past. Don and Sue Clare also decorate their home with antiques. There are old trunks lining the walls and their entertainment center is an antique icebox. Many of the items in the home that are not old appear to be. Sue finds rustic looking décor to accompany the antiques.

Sometimes this antique aesthetic comes with living in the area. Duane, for example, moved to Rabbit Hash originally because of the proximity to the power plant where he works. He has since grown fond of the history and this has led him to shape his life here in Rabbit Hash.

Don, on the other hand, set out with the goal of living in such an area. As a child, he was always interested in steamboats, the river, and pioneers and had the life-long dream of living along the Ohio River in a log cabin. He achieved that goal by taking apart, tagging, moving, and rebuilding the Big Jimmy Ryle house. The home now stands atop a hill overlooking the Ohio River, approximately seven miles from where it originally stood on Beech Grove Road at the top of what is referred to as Big Jimmy Hill. Don is not the only member of the community who moved and rebuilt old log cabins in the Rabbit Hash area. Other than the one that he lives in, there are at least eight in the area. One of these cabins is Duane's. Duane states, "I can't stand to see something torn down and not reused." He made a home out of different parts of different homes from throughout the county.

Jane Burch Cochran, a long time resident of Rabbit Hash and RHHS Board Member, also lives in a log cabin in the area and gives her husband all of the credit for that. He has always been an outdoors enthusiast with an attraction to history and antiques. Over the years, though, she has grown fonder of the idea of living in the cabin and likes the log cabin aesthetic now.

Terrie Markesbery runs the General Store and also lives in a log cabin. She admitted that she and her husband had never really thought of living in a log cabin until they moved to Rabbit Hash. It was contagious,

Don Clare signs paperwork on behalf of the Rabbit Hash Historical Society for the purchase of Rabbit Hash on December 13, 2002. (Photo courtesy of the Clare family)

The Big Jimmy Ryle house that Don Clare tore down and had rebuilt in Rabbit Hash in the early 1980's. (Photo taken by author)

she says, something that she caught when she moved to the area and spent time with other members of the community in their log homes. Throughout the interview, she kept working through possibilities as to why such a trend exists in this particular area. One solution she came up with concerned the landscape. In Texas, where her husband is from, stone houses are common. Kentucky, on the other hand, has trees, so a log cabin maintains a connection to the original landscape of the area. Terrie's theories are supported by the observations often made by scholars of vernacular architecture, food, and folk art which argue that life is shaped by environmental factors, including what is available in a particular area that makes life livable.[9]

Terrie also makes a connection between the rebuilt cabins and the history of the area. She says people are "trying to reconstruct, not just the log house, but the feeling of old times." There is a connection to the history, to the old times, because the structures themselves are old. The cabin also reflects what most of the locals consider a simple lifestyle. The homes have a very basic structure and stand juxtaposed to more modern and complex homes. By building, or re-building log cabins, the Rabbit Hash residents are expressing not only a particular aesthetic but also expressing a different set of values, not based on having the best and most expensive items but instead the more classic and simple items.[10]

Many members of the community also have professions or

hobbies that evince romantic images of the past. In the area are stone carvers, stone masons, blacksmiths, carpenters, and artists who all use traditional methods and styles in their work. The log cabin trend has also made it possible for private builders to specialize in the art of traditional cabin building and rebuilding. Because of the natural environment surrounding Rabbit Hash, there are lots of vegetable gardens and wild game animals, making many members of the community at least partially self-sustaining. Many local men hunt and have an extensive knowledge of guns. This expertise often leads into an aesthetic discussion since some of them make their own guns, most commonly old black powder rifles.

As mentioned before, not everyone moves to Rabbit Hash with this mentality, these hobbies, or these values. Living in this area shapes the lives of its community members, something that they are more than willing to admit. Bobbi Kayser, Rabbit Hash resident and active community member, has lived in Rabbit Hash for ten years. She bought her land before she even knew that the little town of Rabbit Hash was located just over the hill from her new property. However, once she discovered it, she and her children became very interested in the local history and tried to take in as much of it as they could through research, visits to the store and museum, and talking with the old timers in the area. This rich history, she says, "makes you feel like you are really a part of America…you own a piece of America."

Many people also associate living in the area with a natural and simple lifestyle. "It's so simple. It's just so pure and genuine and a simple place to live," Terrie says. Former resident Marlo Thomas associates this simple life with not having to "keep up with the Jones's." Because Rabbit Hash seems to foster an accepting environment, those living in the area are more inclined to cultivate forms of their self-expression. For example, Jane Burch Cochran is an internationally renowned quilter. She gives credit to this lifestyle for changing her work:

> As an artist, it just changed my work totally.... I had the loft in Cincinnati and I was one that grew up with abstract expressionism, paint slinging, you know. And so the artist is supposed to live in a garret and make the world beautiful or crazy by transposing, you know painting on canvases on these large walls.... When you're out here, it's quiet. You have a totally different kind of energy. And I think it can be a deeper thing. You learn to be calmer, hopefully. You can go more into yourself, subconsciously really, and figure out who you are and what your work is. The other thing going on that I think has affected me is that I used to do very abstract work and now I do narrative work and I'm not always sure why.

She has also been told by other artists that she is a storyteller and she feels that too comes with living in a rural setting like Rabbit Hash.

There are some theories that can account for this sort of connection to the history and simplicity of the town. The first of these is in Jean Baudrillard's *The System of Objects*. Baudrillard dedicates a section of this particular work to antiques. "There are two distinctive features of the mythology of the antique object that need to be pointed out: the nostalgia for origins and the obsession with authenticity."[11] He states that we cannot recreate the moment the antique was produced and our knowledge that it has been passed along to many individuals makes the antique seem more authentic. This is very much the case with Rabbit Hash. Looking at the old buildings and the antiques within them connects individuals to something that they cannot ever really experience. Yet knowing what the buildings were used for in the past and knowing about the individuals who built the buildings and operated businesses out of them creates a sense of authenticity. Baudrillard connects the antique to birth, "being born implying, after all, that one has had a father and a mother."[12] There seems to be a loss of that feeling of a homeland in the United States today. People continue to hold on to romantic ideals of what America used to be, the good intentions the country was founded upon, and the strong individuals who once lived here. Yet people also continue to question or doubt our country and compare it to the past. By questioning this, we are losing a connection to our homeland. We can regain this relationship with our motherland by connecting to antiques. When looking at Rabbit Hash, more specifically the General Store, there is no denying that it is old. When people wander in, it takes them back to a time they can never regain, what they see as a true American experience that is rare considering the technological bubble in which most of us spend our time. There are tourist attractions like Colonial Williamsburg and historic tours in most every American city but these are constructed in such a way that the people on the tour, at least subconsciously, know that they are paying for that connection and that that connection is the point of the tour itself. However, in Rabbit Hash, no one is telling you anything or forcing you to relate to specific moments in history. It is up to the individual to use the ambiance of the town, the buildings, the antiques, and the community to shape his or her own authentic relationship with the past.

Another possible explanation for the effect of Rabbit Hash on people living there and visiting is displaced meaning. In his chapter entitled "The Evocative Power of Things", Grant McCracken uses the term "displaced meaning" to describe the gap between the real and the ideal.[13] Basically, what we have and experience daily is not the ideal. The ideal always seems just out of our reach, in "an almost infinite number of locations on the continua of time and place."[14] Rabbit Hash is an example of how ideals can be removed to another time, more specifically a golden age. This golden age is "a largely fictional moment in which social life is imagined to have conformed perfectly to cultural ideals" and to provide "a safe haven for cherished ideals."[15] This, again, refers back to the ideal small-town American community of the past where everyone knew everyone and was willing to help neighbors and friends.

McCracken also argues that "goods serve as bridges"[16] between the real and ideal. Whether its owners are conscious of it or not, the Rabbit Hash General Store contains many goods that serve exactly that purpose. First, and most significant, is the Coca-Cola sign. The focal point of the town is most definitely the front of the General Store. It is a white building and the only pop of color anywhere on it is the large chunk of red under the "Rabbit Hash General Store" sign with white letters that say Coca-Cola in the traditional, easily recognized font. The red makes a sort of arrow that points to a picture of one of the old Coca-Cola advertising characters, Sprite, with his bow tie and bottle cap hat. Before one even enters the store, the tone has been set with this nationally recognized consumer product. I feel that this is the actual current purpose of the sign, rather than an advertisement for Coke, because this style of Coca-Cola advertisement connotes American pastimes and icons such as baseball, movie stars, flappers, and even women's liberation. This concept and the nostalgia surrounding Coke has been the topic of many books. According to Pendegrast, Coke was "advertised as a great national drink, a wholesome, enjoyable product which all classes of Americans could share."[17] Another even discusses the character known as Sprite: Sprite was drawn by Haddon Sundblom, the man also responsible for creating the Santa Claus that America gladly accepts as our most recognizable Christmas icon.[18] Therefore, the artwork also serves a purpose. Since it resembles the style of such an important cultural icon as Santa, those viewing it can associate it with feelings similar to those of a happy Christmas or childhood. This sign is therefore a bridge that takes the viewer to an ideal time that no may longer exist.

Inside the store, there are many items that also serve the purpose of a bridge. One of these is, of course, Coke itself. There are many old Coke bottles around the store that have been there for decades. There is also an old Coke cooler that holds small eight-ounce glass bottles of Coke. The shape of the bottle and the feel of the glass take the consumer back in time, again to a golden, innocent age where there was nothing more enjoyable than a Coke.

Terrie also talked with me about the other products she tries to carry in the store. She is constantly looking for unique things and uses the "tobacco, sundries, notions, and potions" slogan on the Rabbit Hash General Store sign as a guideline for what she keeps in stock at the store. It is important to her to have products that have been around for a long

The Coca-Cola sign has been an iconic piece of the Rabbit Hash General Store for many years and reminds viewers of a golden American past. (Photo taken by author)

Old Coca-Cola products found in the General Store and now on display.
(Photo taken by author)

time such as natural remedies. My experience working in the store has taught me that older generations expect to find certain salves or products in the store because it was something that general stores carried when they were younger. When they do find a particular product, they will purchase it to take them back to that period in their life. Blackjack gum is another such product that I have heard many customers point out and explain that they remember from their past. Most of them don't purchase the gum, but its visual image and presence serves the same function as if they were actually chewing it.

Other than old-fashioned products, local products are also important. People visiting the area enjoy taking something with them that will keep them connected to the town. Here displaced meaning works over space rather than time. Anything that says "Rabbit Hash, Kentucky" is a guaranteed hot item, along with food, candy, and drinks that are made in Kentucky. Many of those who live in Rabbit Hash buy all of the Rabbit Hash products to wear proudly to advertise their hometown or to give as gifts.

Rabbit Hash is a town with a rich history that infiltrates the lives of the people living there. The residents know about and interpret the past, using that interpretation to shape their lives into what is perceived by them, and visitors to the area, to be in congruence with what is a traditional American existence. These efforts have been recognized and perpetuate the town's preservation of history, ambiance, and integrity. While the town has changed immensely over its 180 years, the efforts put forth in the 1970's have made Rabbit Hash into what it is today: a way of connecting to values associated with the past in America, one of these values being a strong and dependable community.

---

[1] My background is in the field of folklore where terms such as history, tradition, heritage, community, festival, authenticity, and performance are often contested and debated. When these terms appear in this work, they are to be taken generally and are used primarily because these are the terms often used by the media, residents, and visitors of Rabbit Hash when discussing and describing the town. It is not my goal to debate the meanings of these words within the pages of this book but rather to use these words as my informants use them to understand and shape their daily lives and perceptions of the town and its image.

[2] Clare, Callie, Caitlyn Clare, and Donald Clare, Jr., "The History of Rabbit Hash," in *Ancestry: Our Ohio River Heritage* (Mt. Vernon, IN: Windmill Publications, Inc., 1996), 24-66.

[3] Yealey, A.M, *History of Boone County, Kentucky: Reprint of Articles Published in Newspapers Over a Period of Fifty Years* (Covington, KY: c1960), 17.

[4] Rennick, Robert M., *From Red Hot to Monkey's Eyebrow: Unusual Kentucky Place Names* (Lexington: University Press of Kentucky, 1997), 34.

[5] Mary Draper Ingles is a well-known heroine in the Northern Kentucky area because Big Bone Lick, just down river from Rabbit Hash, is thought to be the point of her escape from Indians who captured her from her home in Virginia. By following the Ohio, Kanawha, and New Rivers, she eventually made her way back home. Her journey has been made famous through many different retellings of her tale.

[6] Lents, R.V., et al, *Now and Then* (Walton, KY: Walton Advertiser, 1977), 92.

[7] Nelson, William H., *The Buried Treasure: A Rabbit Hash Mystery* (Mt. Vernon, IN: Windmill Publications, Inc., 1997), 17-20.

[8] Clare, "The History of Rabbit Hash," 60.

[9] For example, see works such as Brown, Linda Keller and Kay Mussell, eds., *Ethnic and Regional Foodways in the United States: The Performance of Group Identity* (Knoxville: University of Tennessee Press, 1984); Burrison, John, *Roots of a Region: Southern Folk Culture* (Jackson: University of Mississippi Press); Glassie, Henry, *Material Culture* (Bloomington: Indiana University Press, 1999); and Roberts, Warren E., *Log Buildings of Southern Indiana* (Bloomington: Trickster Press, 1996).

[10] See Glassie, Henry, "The Appalachian Log Cabin," in *Baseball, Barns, and Bluegrass: A Geography of American Folklife*, Ed. George O. Carnery (New York: Rowman and Littlefield Publishers, Inc., 1998), 19-28.

[11] Baudrillard, Jean. *The System of Objects*. Trans. James Benedict (New York: Verso, 2005), 80.

[12] Ibid., 20.

[12] McCracken, Grant, "The Evocative Power of Things: Consumer Goods and the Preservation of Hopes and Ideals," in *Culture and Consumption: New Approaches to the Symbolic Character of Consumer Goods and Activities* (Bloomington: Indiana University Press, 1988), 104-117.

[14] Ibid., 106.

[15] Ibid., 106.

[16] Ibid., 105.

[17] Pendergrast, Mark, *For God, Country and Coca-Cola: The Definitive History of the Great American Soft Drink and the Company that Makes It* (New York: Basic Books, 2000).

[18] Shartar, Martin and Norman Shavin, *The Wonderful World of Coca-Cola* (Atlanta: Capricorn Corporation, Inc., 1981).

CHAPTER II: A SMALL-TOWN COMMUNITY

One very important aspect of Rabbit Hash is its community. Without many generations of dedicated community members, Rabbit Hash would not have survived into the new millennium. This chapter is for them, the Rabbit Hash locals who maintain the appeal and way of life of the town. To be considered a local, one does not necessarily have to live in Rabbit Hash's tiny downtown. If that were the case, only Louie, who is currently Rabbit Hash's only official resident, would be the only local. This group is mostly made up of the people who live in the areas surrounding Rabbit Hash. With very little else in the area, Rabbit Hash becomes the center of social life for those living in the area.

Those that make up the Rabbit Hash community are all very similar, yet at the same time, quite diverse. With very few exceptions, the community members share the same rural Caucasian background. However, many of the locals are also extremely progressive demonstrating equality between men and women and tolerance for different groups and lifestyles. What does vary quite a bit is age, career, and years spent living in the area. Community members range from small children to individuals in their eighties and nineties, from farmers and laborers to CEO's and inventors, and from those that have lived in the area all their lives to people recently moving in from as far away as Los Angeles and Canada.

For the most part, all of these different types of people blend well together and travel in the same circles regardless of these differences that may have kept them separate elsewhere. However, like any group of people, tensions do arise with differing opinions on how the town should be run or even over more personal matters and meaningless gossip. While these disputes can hinder some community relationships, they tend to be worked out or forgotten quickly. It appears that the members of the Rabbit Hash community strive to make it conform to the image of the ideal small country town where everyone knows your name, is willing to help, and works together.

What Makes a Community?

During my interviews, I asked everyone what they considered to be the most valued aspect of life in Rabbit Hash. An overwhelming number of them responded with one word, "community."[1] Yet this community is something that doesn't just happen because the town is secluded and has a long history of a strong community. It is something that must be actively maintained by those living in the area and many people dedicate quite a bit of time into organizing and hosting community events. There are many reasons why everyone assigns such great value to the community and work so hard to maintain it. Living in Rabbit Hash ensures that one is at least a half hour away from anything else. There are no high schools, shopping centers, malls, bars, cafes, or restaurants for miles. But what Rabbit Hash does have is the General Store. "You know everybody, especially if you go in the General Store for any length of time. You'll eventually see everybody," says Sue Clare. She even refers to the General Store as the "lifeline of the town."

Because everyone seems to remain connected through this old General Store and the three and a half acres surrounding it, those that spend time at the General Store do so purposefully so that they may remain connected to others as well as to the history of the town. It is more convenient and comforting to have a place near one's home where individuals can meet and build relationships with others who live nearby and on whom they can grow to rely. Whether consciously or because the Rabbit Hash lifestyle lends itself to this particular type of community, Rabbit Hash represents the close-knit, ideal society that the people in Rabbit Hash associate with traditional values of the small-town American past: close relationships, sharing and help during hard times, coming together in celebration, trust, safety, teaching the next generation, and inclusion.

One of these aspects of community that most of my interviewees at least mentioned is the fact that everyone knows everyone else and that contributes to the town's charm. You know everyone's business and, unfortunately, what comes with that is everyone knowing yours. While

The Rabbit Hash General Store is the center of community life in Rabbit Hash and is where locals gather for all occasions. (Photo taken by author)

Reverend Tinkle preaching on the porch of the General Store in 1918. (Courtesy of the Rabbit Hash Historical Society)

gossip and having no secrets is something that is bothersome at times, according to Sue Clare, people will also leave you to your peace and quiet. However, they are always helpful and many times you don't even have to ask. Sue spoke of times when people came to our family's aid. When her husband and my father, Don, had a heart attack, one of the men from the town brought us a load of firewood for the wood burning stove, the major source of heat in the home. When my grandmother died, Carleen Stephens brought a tray of food to us as a gift from the East Bend Baptist Church, a church that our family doesn't even attend. And every year when there is a major snow, our neighbors plow our driveway for us without even telling us they'll be there.

Everyone that I interviewed had stories like this to demonstrate the closeness of the community. Leslie Green mentions how locals have helped her by fixing her cars for her and checking out the electricity in a home that she was thinking about buying. When others in the community have work to do on their homes, when a pet or family member dies, or when someone needs to borrow anything, there are many individuals nearby willing to help.

Rabbit Hash community events are the best examples of how the residents come together for a common goal. The Old Timers Day celebration (detailed in the next chapter) requires many helping hands as do the events held by the Rabbit Hash Historical Society to raise money

Leslie enjoying an evening after work on the porch of the General Store.
(Photo taken by author)

Tommy sits around the stove in the General Store after work. (Photo taken by the author)

for town upkeep. Tommy, one of the locals who has spent his whole life in Rabbit Hash, is always willing to cook for the events and Duane Doyle is more than willing to clean up the town, keep the grass mowed, and set up tents, tables, and chairs.

In 2007 after one of the locals became very ill, many individuals in the community came together to form the Friends of Rabbit Hash and organized a huge benefit. The success of the benefit gave the Friends of Rabbit Hash the momentum to continue endeavors to help others in need and have been organizing fundraising and community events since.

Perhaps the most trusting example of community and sharing is exhibited by Terrie Markesbery, proprietor of the General Store, in the form of tabs. While the Rabbit Hash General Store does do a decent business, it is still a risky move on that of the business owner to allow individuals, in this case the locals, to run a tab at the store. The tab is a remnant of the General Store's business operation that has remained intact since its beginning. It is a tradition that simply carries over with each business owner. Of course there are some requirements for this privilege: Terrie must know the individual well and for an extended period of time before they can run a tab. Being able to open a tab after moving to the community or spending more and more time in the General Store is a rite of passage. It signifies more than the false satisfaction of getting something for nothing. Rather it signifies trust and acceptance into the

Duane chats with other locals on the porch of the General Store on a weekday after work. (Photo taken by author)

Terrie Markesbery, current proprietor of the Rabbit Hash General Store, in the front entrance of the store. (Photo courtesy of Terrie Markesbery)

community. It also sets these individuals apart from visitors as they often skip the line at the register calling out, "Put it on my tab," as they walk past.

An important aspect that contributes to the sense of community in any location and that parents appreciate a great deal is the satisfying feeling they get knowing that their children are safe and cared for. Marlo, Leslie, and Bobbi were all single mothers when they moved to the area and in Rabbit Hash they found the support and help needed to raise their children. According to Bobbi, it was "a village raising the children.... You want to give them more than just a subdivision or a school. You want to give them a sense of real belonging as they're growing up, especially when you are a single mom." This sense of belonging was possible in Rabbit Hash where all of the kids in the area numbered their moms. Their biological mom was always Mom #1 while the other women would be Mom #2 or Mom #3. There was always a mom around to watch what was going on, pass out punishments, and pass out love. In many ways, the kids in the area seem to have lots of freedom because of the overwhelming presence of motherhood in this community. "I know who they're with. Or they can walk down the road with friends. If they get picked up I understand that they're going to be okay because they know who to go with and who not to go with and that's kinda cool when you're a parent," says Marlo. Leslie shared a similar sentiment. She likes the fact that she can still have a social life, and her children can be a part of it. By going to the General Store on Friday and Saturday nights, she was able to have the best of both worlds: time with friends and time with her children. Terrie shares this sentiment. When asked what she finds so special about the town and the community, she responded, "It's a safe place to raise my kid, a place where other people are helping me raise my kid." She also feels fortunate that there is always someone around who her daughter knows and who will watch out for her. All of the mothers I interviewed are glad that Rabbit Hash is where they are raising or raised their children. My interview with Sue Clare, my mother, ended with her comment, "I have no regrets moving here and raising you and [your sister] here because I think you've both turned out pretty darn good."

Of course this closeness and reliance on one another depends on the individuals living in the area, and according to many locals Rabbit Hash attracts some very interesting types of people that foster this lifestyle of acceptance. According to Jane Burch Cochran, who has lived in the area for over thirty years and now serves on the Rabbit Hash Historical Society Board, "We like crazies." As funny as this statement sounds, it is very true of Rabbit Hash. Jane continues by saying, "I do think that people are pretty accepting of you and they're also pretty accepting of other people that would not fit in other parts of society. Well, they accept the town drunk so to speak.... And I love individual

kind of people which I think you probably do too from living out here."
Bobbi adds, "Everybody down here knows they belong."

Many of the people I interviewed also referred to how people
who live in Rabbit Hash don't feel the same pressures as those living in
other areas. Because Boone County is one of the fastest growing counties
in Kentucky, there are subdivisions popping up on many of the old farms.
These subdivisions became a point of comparison in many of the
interviews. There are no rules for landscaping and behavior in Rabbit
Hash, as there are in subdivisions. There is more freedom in Rabbit Hash.
As I mentioned in the previous chapter, there is no need to keep up with
the Jones'. "I don't think anybody really cares around here," says Marlo.
Leslie told me that she wouldn't feel free to be herself in the suburbs,
where there is a feeling of being judged. Whether or not it is the freedom
that attracts the unique individuals or the individuals who foster the
freedom to be oneself, no one is sure but the two are undeniably linked
and encouraged.

Also, in contrast to subdivisions, especially those referred to as
"planned communities," the locals find their community to be a genuine
community. Calling an area a "planned community" implies that once a
family moves in, they will immediately be accepted into a pre-existing
community and will embrace a certain set of pre-determined standards.
The Rabbit Hash locals are skeptical of this way of life. Tommy says:

[Rabbit Hash is] not like... a planned community where they come in and bulldoze a farm and build houses and build a clubhouse in the center of it and expect these people to get along well.... Like all these people are supposed to gather around there and consider themselves a community and in all reality, a community like that, those people they don't know. One guy he probably doesn't even know his neighbor's last name or he might not even know what he does for a living. He knows nothing about him. Whereas around here you know who's who and what they do and whether you can trust them or not.

Duane Doyle adds to the subdivision discussion by talking about how the subdivisions are advertised as being in a rural setting. He mentions reading about how a builder was building 147 homes on fifty-one acres but maintaining a green space all around in order to give the subdivision a rural feel. Because these are being built in what was once rural Kentucky, there is an effort for them to somehow remain connected to the land on which they are built and they are given names like Farmview and Hempsteade, after what was destroyed to make them. Therefore, one of the perks of living in Rabbit Hash is its "real" rural setting surrounded by nature and farms, a perfect setting for a simple and fulfilling life.

Who are the Locals?

As mentioned previously, the residents of Rabbit Hash are
somewhat homogenous in ethnic background. Besides that, however, the
community is quite diverse and this does not go unnoticed by the locals.
"I like the mix of people," states Duane, "not that you agree with
everybody of course, you know, because that's impossible. It's just there's
such a wide variety; farmers to millionaires and artists and everything in
between." Here, Duane mentions perhaps the most obvious difference
among the residents and that is socioeconomic class. Rabbit Hash attracts
some wealthy individuals who build very expensive homes right next to
the more modest homes of individuals who have lived in the area for a
much longer period of time. While a majority of what is presented to us in
popular culture seems to pretend that we live in a classless society and
fails to address the differences between the classes, economic distinctions
are superficially obvious in Rabbit Hash. No one really addresses class
unless provoked, not because the community pretends that there is no
difference, but because it is not seen as an issue. No one fails to associate
with another person based on class.

Another obvious difference that exists among the members of
the community is age. It is common for communities to have members of

all ages and Rabbit Hash is no exception. It is the way in which the different age groups interact in Rabbit Hash that is unique. Within the visible locals, a group discussed at length below, the individuals range from young children up to people in their eighties. Despite age, everyone is treated as a friend and the common tenets of age are disregarded. Leslie was very interested in this aspect of the community, finding it to be something unique to Rabbit Hash. "I don't really think there's many places that you have that many age groups where we can all actually party together and hang out."

One way in which I differentiate between residents of Rabbit Hash is based on what percentages of their lifetimes have been spent living in the town and when they moved to the area. Based on this criteria, I have come up with three different categories, but these remain quite fluid since there are individuals that don't necessarily fall into just one. The first of these groups that I have identified consists of those who have lived in Rabbit Hash their entire lives. When Don first started collecting the oral history of the town, these are the people that he went to, the old timers. Don remembers talking with Robert Hayden Wilson (the grandson of James A. Wilson who first ran the General Store), who he refers to as "the most colorful" man in town. Robert told Don many different stories about how Rabbit Hash and it community used to be. One story he told was about the two churches and the two stores. There are two churches very close to Rabbit Hash and they are less than a half mile away from one another: the East Bend Baptist Church (which still holds three services a week) and the East Bend Methodist Church (which has not held services for at least thirty years, but the building is currently owned and maintained by the Rabbit Hash Historical Society). Robert referred to the churches as "the white church," East Bend Baptist, and "the red church," East Bend Methodist (based on the color of each building) and told Don that in the past which church an individual went to on Sunday determined if one shopped at the Ryle Brothers' Store or the Rabbit Hash General Store, then known as the Stephen's General Store. Mimicking Robert's voice, Don adds, "Why on Saturdays, they'd gather at the store and talk religion and then on Sunday they'd gather outside the church and talk politics." Don explains that at that time there were no social castes based on class because everyone was a farmer earning close to the same amount of money. Instead, they would create castes based upon political or religious affiliations. While there was no rift between the two groups, it was a way for them to help define themselves through oppositions in a community where there were no real differences.

Now, most of the old timers have passed away and many others of the next generation have moved away making it more difficult to find people that have lived in the area their entire lives. Today, Bob is one of the oldest town residents and has spent all but four of his eighty-three

East End Baptist Church (the White Church). (Photo taken by author)

East Bend Methodist Church (the Red Church). (Photo taken by author)

years in Rabbit Hash. Those four years away were spent in the Marine Corps fighting in the Korean War. Bob also has family in the area; Tommy is the son of Bob's cousin and has been to several different states for long periods of time for work. However, he always returns to Rabbit Hash. "It's where I grew up, you know, all I know. I've been other places but just always wind up back here…These are the people that I know and they're my type of people. To me, it's a way of life." Carleen Stephens and her husband have also lived their entire lives in Rabbit Hash. Carleen was born on Lower River Road and when she got married moved to her husband's farm, also on Lower River Road. She says she has stayed in Rabbit Hash all her sixty-two years because of the community. She also serves as a member of the RHHS Board, helping to preserve the town in which she has lived her entire life. "I like the sense of community. Everybody knew everybody, everybody helped everybody."

According to Carleen, the Rabbit Hash General Store, along with the two churches, has always been the center of the community. Don agrees stating that the store has been the "pulse of this civic area all its life. No matter what generation, you hung out at the store. It's where people socialized or talked."[2]

The store is definitely the center of the world for a second type of local. Today, this group sometimes considers itself the new old timers since they have been slowly becoming some of the oldest people living in

Bob heading into the General Store for his Friday night shift. (Photo taken by author)

Carleen Stephens, life-long resident of Rabbit Hash and member of the Rabbit Hash Historical Society, playing piano at the East Bend Baptist Church.
(Photo courtesy of Carleen Stephens)

the area. However, they are people who weren't born and raised in Rabbit Hash but moved into the area in the 60's, 70's, and 80's. This coincided with Louie Scott buying up the buildings in Rabbit Hash. My father, Don, was a musician, and one of the roadies for his band moved to Ryle Road, about ten miles from Rabbit Hash. My parents often went to this rural area of Boone County to visit and there they also met Jane Cochran, her husband, and Louie. When Louie bought the property in Rabbit Hash and was sleeping in the General Store, many of the men would collect there on Friday nights and drink whiskey while discussing possible plans for the town. These were also referred to as "Historical Society Meetings." Of course then everyone wanted to move to Rabbit Hash. Don went door to door looking for land to buy so that he could live along the Ohio River. Eventually he met Beulah Riggs, an elderly widow with a large farm. While she said she wasn't going to sell, she allowed Don to camp on her land. Eventually they became friends and when she decided to sell, Don and a friend purchased the farm together, each getting about 35 acres. Sue Clare associates this movement with a post-hippie era. She says that in college these individuals were the hippies and after college they were looking for something different, a way to live off of the earth and be self-sufficient. Today this generation has been in Rabbit Hash the longest, some nearly fifty years. They mixed well with the old timers when they moved in and worked to keep the town going. They also used to be the locals that were seen at the General Store daily working or just hanging out around the stove. However, today they aren't as present as they once were, having passed the torch and turf to the next generation of locals.

The last category of local consists of those who have moved into the area fairly recently. There are many reasons for people moving to Rabbit Hash. For older residents, it is usually a place for them to spend their retirement. For some of the younger people, it is the closeness of the community that draws them to the area. Many of them, like Leslie Green, who has lived in the area for about ten years, spent time in Rabbit Hash before ever thinking of moving to the area. Making friends, finding relationships, wanting to get away from the city, and wanting a safe place for their children to grow up are all reasons that bring this group to the area. Marlo Thomas who lived in the area for about seven years was a tourist on a motorcycle the first time she visited Rabbit Hash. She became friends with many of the people in the area and began to visit Rabbit Hash more frequently, even bringing her children who also met new friends. Eventually she moved to the area and still visits town regularly.

Activity in the Town

Again, despite many similarities, there is no doubt that the community is quite diverse. This is something that all of my interviewees attempted to express. Jane referred to it as a microcosm of the world.

There is a wide range of socioeconomic classes that intermingle on a regular basis, as well as many age groups. This is most evident in one more category of local that I did not include in the original three categories I discussed because it is made up of members of each of the other three. This is the group that I have come to refer to as the "visible locals." These are the people who any visitor to the town is likely to see in the General Store, sitting on the porch, or outside. This is also the group of the Rabbit Hash locals who are the closest to one another. They see each other almost every day and at times appear to travel in packs.

Being from Rabbit Hash doesn't necessarily ensure that you are one of these locals. Certain things are expected of you; you must attend all major Rabbit Hash events and be seen around town most weekends. In fact, living in Rabbit Hash doesn't even seem to be a requirement. There are many individuals who don't live in the Rabbit Hash area but are in town more than many residents. Not only do they spend lots of time in the town, they add to the sense of community by helping out other members and actively working to preserve the town.

This segment of the population is most evident on the weekends. The nature of the weekend activities differs depending on the season. During the winter, tourists are scarce. From Friday evening until Sunday evening, the town belongs to the locals. After finishing up work for the week, people begin to file into the General Store. Although the sign says

Locals gather behind the stove in the Rabbit Hash General Store to play music on a Friday evening. (Photo taken by author)

The crowd gathers around the Whiskey Bent Valley Boys at the General Store. (Photo taken by author)

that the store closes at seven, rules are bent. The locals gather in the store around the wood stove discussing the events of the week or some even play music. There is always a group on the front porch multi-tasking as both smokers and sentries. Surveys are taken: who drives by and doesn't stop, how many unrecognized vehicles pass, where so-and-so could be going. There is one requirement if you expect the store to stay open late, or at all, and that is to support the local economy, most commonly fulfilled by the purchase of a twelve-pack or series of twenty-two ounce beers.

Most Fridays, a few people will bring large pots of food of something warm and easy to make to share with everyone else. On these nights, the store stays open late, especially if there are a few people playing music around the stove. Even after the store closes around 10:00, many people don't want the evening to end, but no one wants to drive too far from home. One of the locals will step up and invite the others to his or her home for an end of the evening party.

Saturdays are quite similar to Fridays, but begin much earlier. Having worked in the store, I began to recognize patterns. To use an example, one of the locals typically came to the store shortly after opening to buy a caffeinated drink to begin the day. A few hours later, he would be back for a snack and a soda. Then around three or four, he would return, takes his coveralls off and buy a twenty-two-ounce beer indicating that his

The Downtown County Band performs on the front porch of the General Store.
(Photo taken by author)

A crowd waits outside the barn for the barn dance music to begin. (Photo taken by author)

day of chores was done and he had settled into the store for the rest of the evening. After five or six on a cold Saturday, the only people who come into the store are locals, again slowly filing in after the day's tasks have been completed or when the effects of Friday's over-imbibing have been properly nursed.

The community gathers again on Sunday when individuals come in for morning coffee and then gather in the mid-afternoon to enjoy the "Sundays behind the Stove" musical entertainment. For these Sundays Terrie invites various bands from the Cincinnati area down to play music. The bands bring a larger crowd with them and their purchases help the store through the financially difficult winter months. Terrie brings in bluegrass, rockabilly, blues, Cajun, or any other type of music she feels fits the Rabbit Hash environment.

The summers in Rabbit Hash are much busier for the General Store and the more pleasant weather means that more people gather in Rabbit Hash every day of the week, not just on the weekends. On the warm summer evenings after work most of the locals will pass through Rabbit Hash for a drink and to see who else is around. Some nights there is no one around other than the store operator, but on other nights the whole town might be present. Since it stays light until nearly 10:00 pm, the locals lose track of time and stay sitting around the picnic tables a little longer than intended. The store won't stay open much past seven o'clock

Dancers occupy the space closest to the band while other people look on from the back and sides of the barn. (Photo taken by author)

Tubs of beverages are put on ice in preparation for the barn dance crowd. (Photo taken by author)

since everyone sits outside but whoever is running the store will stand out on the front porch and yell out "Last call!" to make sure no one misses making a necessary purchase.

The weekends are very similar. Town fills up on Friday evenings with most people sitting outside rather than in. The chances of having visitors in town are greater when the weather is nicer. One Friday night a month, there is a barn dance. Quite often the bands that play the barn dances are the same bands that play the Sunday music. Music starts at 7:00 pm and goes until 10:00 with the barn full of people and food. Terrie moves much of her beer and soft drink stock to the barn to sell during the dance. When the barn doors close, there is sometimes a fire on the river bank, but often the party continues at someone's home. Saturdays and Sundays are very crowded with motorcycles and tourists during the summer, and the locals tend to avoid sitting in town when their usual spots are occupied by strangers. Some days the picnic tables or one of the yards in Rabbit Hash is the gathering point, but often times everyone collects at someone's home or even on someone's boat.

These weekends in Rabbit Hash exist as a liminoid[3] space for the Rabbit Hash locals because it suspends their ordinary lives. Although Rabbit Hash is still very much a part of 'normal society,' it is somewhat outside of it. Everything considered 'normal,' such as jobs and weekly responsibilities, are at least twenty miles away. The weekends, when the

A usual warm Sunday afternoon crowd in Rabbit Hash. (Photo taken by author)

locals don't have to leave the comfort of Rabbit Hash if they don't want to, serve as a break from the day to day routine. During the weekends, a strong collectivism is exhibited by the locals: many of them are together every day for socializing and relieving the stress of the work-week. Locals are free to be themselves with no concern for rules of propriety enforced in normal society. However, the weekends always end, which makes them liminoid. The drive home on Friday afternoons is the transition from individual in normal society to part of a 'we' in the liminal society. The winding down on Sunday evenings marks a transition from the social member of 'we' back into the individual with responsibilities in the 'real world' outside of Rabbit Hash. There is a constant back and forth between the two worlds making it impossible to become fully part of just one. There is never a complete transition from individual to 'we' or from 'we' to individual. It is also during liminal times that a society's deepest values emerge[4]. In Rabbit Hash these values are clearly the close-knit community and the ideal small-town America.

But Nothing's Perfect

Thus far, I have made it appear that Rabbit Hash is an idyllic community. That, however, is not always the case. With diversity, there is sure to be some adversity. This came to a head in 2003 after the Rabbit Hash Historical Society took over the town. When Louie owned the town, there was really not much concern with how the town was being run since the property belonged to a private individual. But when the RHHS took over ownership, some residents assumed they were a city council. Sue Clare, member of the RHHS, says, "For some reason people think we can make rules or laws." The main goal of the RHHS is to preserve the historic integrity of the town. Because they are now the owners of the town, they are also responsible for town maintenance, collecting rent, and paying bills. And while all major decisions regarding the town are in the hands of the RHHS, they cannot give into or accommodate all grievances, complaints, and suggestions (although they will try). Most of the complaints are with traffic and too many cars and motorcycles in town, something that the RHHS has no control over and would also not like to discourage; many cars mean many people coming to and appreciating the town for its many merits.

There has also been some tension between the visible locals and those that have made the choice to not be an active member of the Rabbit Hash community and who moved to the area for peace and quiet. Tommy sums up his side of the case:

> They want it to be like a picture post card place where
> the good ole boy can't come down here and sit and hang
> out. They want it to look like a Norman Rockwell picture
> so that when, on occasion, they do have a friend come in

from town and visit they can come down here and buy them an ice-cream and a candy bar and say, "Look we live in this little quaint town that don't change by time and nothing ever happens here. It's so quiet and peaceful here."

But according to him and the others I've talked with who have spent their entire lives in Rabbit Hash, the way the visible locals use the General Store now is how they've always used it, since 1831. The people who are newer to the area have a different idea of preservation, one that is more concerned with preserving the parts of America that speak to our nostalgic tendencies; they are after a more romanticized version of the past and a simple way of life. The visible locals want the America that stresses the importance of community and allows for them to get away with things that are taboo in the city or suburbs.

These conflicting ideals of what Rabbit Hash should be will probably never be resolved but there have been efforts on part of the Rabbit Hash Historical Society and the Friends of Rabbit Hash to host community events and to invite everyone who lives in the area. These have turned out well and things have calmed down quite a bit over the past several years.

While the perfect society or community can never be realized[5], it can be imagined. The members of the Rabbit Hash community may all have a different image of the perfect community but that does not keep them from striving for it, something they feel can be more easily achieved in Rabbit Hash than in suburban communities. Rabbit Hash may come across as idealized yet the locals have managed to make it into a place where the members of the community are not only treated as, but are, equals. Like any society, there are those with more than others; these differences are expressed by the jobs people have and even the cars they drive. Although it is known that there are certain stratifications among the group members, it does not hinder the socializing or sense of equality within the group.

The residents of Rabbit Hash work to construct and maintain a strong sense of community, which they perceive as a central feature of a traditional rural American small-town way of life they want to preserve or recreate in Rabbit Hash.

---

[1] Because this is the term used by those living in the area, it is also the word that I have chosen to use when writing about the town's residents. Therefore, "community" is being used in a very basic sense of the word. To read more on the contested definitions and weight of this word in previous Folklore scholarship, please see works such as Glassie, Henry, *The Stars of Ballymenone* (Bloomington: Indiana University Press), 2006 and Feintuch, Burt, "Longing for Community" in *Western Folklore* 60 (2001): 149-161.

[2] Many scholars have pointed out the need for an important gathering place for the growth and maintenance of a close community. See Glassie, *The Stars of Ballymenone*, 25 for a discussion of the role of the ceili in the Irish town of Ballymenone.

[3] This is in opposition to the liminal space which changes things. See Turner, *The Anthropology of Performance* and Kamau, Lucy Jayne, "Liminality, Communitas, Charisma, and Community," in *Intentional Community: An Anthropological Perspective*, ed. Susan Love Brown (Albany: State University of New York Press, 2002), 17-40.

[4] Turner, *The Anthropology of Performance*, 102.

[5] Turner, *The Anthropology of Performance*, 84.

CHAPTER III: OLD TIMERS DAY

Rabbit Hash, Kentucky has experienced a growth in popularity over the years. What was once an old town that Sunday drivers found by accident is now a thriving tourist destination with a strong sense of community. This popularity has taken Rabbit Hash from the realm of the private, a small and intimate community, and opened it up to the public. Though visible on the weekends, this transition is most evident on the Saturday before Labor Day each year at the annual "Old Timers Day"[1] celebration.

Old Timers Day is the closest thing to a ritual or festival to take place in Rabbit Hash and functions as a "communal celebration[2]." This was its initial purpose, but today Old Timers Day is no longer an intimate gathering of neighbors. It now more closely resembles a public display event since it has more active participation in a variety of different genres and activities such as contest, food, drink, music, dance, arts, and crafts[3]. Of course how Old Timers Day functions and what it means differs from group to group and even from person to person, depending on the type of relationships each has with the festival. Participants can range from organizers, visible locals, and residents to tourists and regular visitors[4]. Therefore, what exactly is being celebrated (history, community, food, music, the end of summer) is not the same for everyone. In response to

The cake commemorating the very first Old Timers Day celebration in Rabbit Hash on July 5, 1980. (Photo courtesy of the Clare family)

Bill Stephens (center), long-time resident of Rabbit Hash, provided valuable oral history to the Rabbit Hash Historical Society. Here, Bill speaks to other residents at the first Old Timers Day. (Photo courtesy of the Clare family)

these differences, the Rabbit Hash Historical Society attempts to maintain some elements of tradition and reminders of what the festival originally meant to the community. Many strive to keep Old Timers Day as a way to celebrate the town's past, community and continued preservation even though both the town and the event are constantly changing and evolving into something much different.

Old Timers Day began in 1980 and was held over Fourth of July weekend in the old blacksmith shop across the street from the General Store. The store remained open and served as the watering hole for the party. Old Timers Day's sole purpose was to bring the Rabbit Hash community together. According to Don Clare, Louie Scott started Old Timers Day because "he still had that sense of community." Don continues:

> He started this thing that he called Old Timers Day where he'd invite all the area residents downtown for a day of visiting.... It was a big social for people who lived here, people who used to live here.

Sue Clare adds that Louie "kept saying he wanted all the old timers to get together and tell stories about growing up in Rabbit Hash." He invited everyone living in Rabbit Hash and others that had grown up in the area but had since moved away. "Everybody would sit around and talk all day long and tell stories and take pictures," says Sue. Many would also bring

From right to left: Brandon Scott, Louie Scott, and Gary "Whiteman" White prepare food for the first Old Timers Day celebration. (Photo courtesy of the Clare family)

Rabbit Hash residents gathering at the General Store for the beginning of the first Old Timers Day celebration. (Photo courtesy of the Clare family)

family photos or historical information to share with their neighbors and friends. For some, Old Timers Day even served as a family reunion because it was the one day each year that people who had moved out of the area would return to visit with family and old friends.

The party was a potluck for which Louie provided the meat, designating a few to help cook it, and everyone else brought a dish to share. Carleen Stephens says, "You just told your neighbor to come to Rabbit Hash and bring a dish and we just got together and had a day together." Potlucks reflect the key role community plays because the lack of structure in the meal promotes togetherness among the people in attendance. Everyone is sharing something that they made with everyone else in the ultimate expression of reciprocity and appreciation – food.

The Old Timers Days started early with people beginning to gather downtown in the morning and were continuously joined by others throughout the early afternoon hours. Sue remembers how wonderful it was to see everyone socializing with everyone else despite some very fundamental differences in opinion or lifestyles, such as the Baptists who "would come too and they'd all mingle even though there was drinking, smoking and swearing." Jane Burch Cochran remembers that there wasn't as much going on at the early Old Timers Days as the current ones. People were there for the social aspect and the food. However, in the evening, Don's band would play. The first Old Timers Day was before the

View of the Old Timers Day activity. Residents gathered for a good parking spot.
(Photo courtesy of the Clare family)

Music has always had a place at Old Timers Day with the old blacksmith shop as the stage.
(Photo courtesy of the Clare family)

Rabbit Hash barn was built so the band would play in the blacksmith shop or on the porch of the store. After the barn was built, the band often set up on its porch. Carleen Stephens remembers the old Old Timers Days when she and her husband "used to come up here at 7:30 on a Saturday morning of Old Timers Day and park our truck so we had a place to sit when Donnie and the band started playing."

For the new generation of old timers, these early Old Timers Days were the best. They enjoyed that the day centered on the community and the people living there. The event wasn't advertised or open to the public; it was just for them and the growth of community and the passing on of traditions and stories. However, like most things, Old Timers Day changed. First of all, the date changed. Many people found that the Fourth of July weekend was too hot for sitting outside all day so the event was moved to Labor Day weekend instead. While it still gets quite warm that weekend, it is much cooler than early July. The event also grew as people in the area started to invite their friends and family. Others living nearby, but who were not necessarily part of the community, also began coming and bringing people with them. As it grew, whoever was operating the General Store inherited the responsibilities for organizing the event and each one had their own ideas about how the event should grow. Unfortunately, like anything else, the event depends on money so in order for it to continue, the General Store must make a profit to invest in the following year. In order to make that money off of beverages and souvenirs and still keep admission free, a larger crowd was required. In order to get that crowd, Old Timers Day has been advertised through word of mouth, in local papers, on the internet, and sometimes even on television and radio for several years in the hopes of bringing in a large crowd that will ensure enough profit to fund the celebration the following year.

With more and more people attending Old Timers Day, the potluck became too large to handle. Eventually a ticket system was instituted to guarantee that those who brought a dish would get a meal. Each person with a dish would exchange it at the table for as many tickets as people in their family so they all could eat.

Policies changed with different General Store managers. Jane remembers that when the crowd became overwhelmingly large, the manager of the store in the 1980's and 90's announced that the old timers would be the first to go through the line to get their food. While this act may seem small it meant a lot to Jane because it was a reminder of what the day originally meant to the community.

For several years now, there has been no Old Timers Day potluck because the crowds have been so large and it became too hard to manage. Some people would attend Old Timers Day before knowing much about it and fail to bring food. In order to get tickets for the food line, they would buy chips and dip from the store to pass off as their dish. A larger crowd also meant that people were no longer eating the food made by close friends and neighbors but by strangers, something that concerned many individuals. Judging by the strict health department regulations today, I imagine that if the potluck was still an element of Old Timers Day, the health department would be watching closely and maybe even shutting it down. Terrie Markesbery, the current operator of the General Store, is responsible for making the decision to end the potluck dinner and bring in outside food vendors. Although a very practical solution for the large crowds on Old Timers Day, there exists a sense of loss for the private meal that was once shared by all of the members of the Rabbit Hash community.

As with any public display event, music is a very important element. It draws a large crowd and keeps them entertained. However, this also demonstrates another way in which the day has turned from private to public. Don Clare has lived in the area since the 1970's and was quickly accepted by the locals because of his interest in the town, its history, and its people. Because of this, his band was asked to play the first Old Timers Days. While he was the only member of the band who actually lived in the area, his band mates were also accepted in the community. Danny was a member of the band who also lived in Northern Kentucky and he acted as the emcee for the Old Timers Day events. Jane

The Scalded Hog sets up shop in front on the barn to sell food on Old Timers Day, 2010. (Photo taken by author)

The Downtown County band plays an afternoon set on Old Timers Day, 2010. (Photo taken by author)

refers to Danny as a "hoot" and finds his performance on stage to be one of her fondest memories of the event.

Today, there are many bands that play Old Timers Day, from noon until midnight. However, very rarely do any of these bands have any ties to Rabbit Hash other than it being a trendy venue. While these bands play traditional bluegrass, rockabilly, blues, folk, Cajun, or roots music and appreciate the town for what it is, they are from outside the community and represent the change of this celebration from a private event to one that is more public and less intimate.

Larger crowds also cause more logistical problems, such as lack of parking. Terrie has arranged for parking on private land down either end of Lower River Road. The silent heroes of Old Timers Day are the locals who volunteer to drive a tractor and hay wagon up and down the road all day picking people up after they've parked and returning them to their cars when they are leaving. At any given time, there are several kids on the wagon just enjoying the hayride.

With the bands and the food vendors, the Old Timers Days of today more closely resemble a street fair or festival than a day to remember the history of the town. There are some ways that the connection to history is attempted though. The Rabbit Hash Historical Society has a tiny cabin museum in Rabbit Hash under the best shade tree in town. The museum used to be open every weekend with a volunteer

Two Belgian horses, Jim and Barney, were a valuable addition to the early Old Timers Day celebrations by providing hayrides throughout the day. (Photo courtesy of the Clare family)

Since being built, the Rabbit Hash Historical Society Museum is open each year on Old Timers Day displaying historical photos and information. (Photo courtesy of the Clare family)

sitting outside answering questions and accepting donations. However, as more and more motorcycles came to town, interest in the history of the town waned and transferred to the machines lining the street. This discouraged the RHHS volunteers who dedicated their weekends to opening the museum. Now in order to look through the museum, an appointment is required. Other than by appointment, the only time that the museum is open is on Old Timers Day. The museum is the building farthest away from the General Store, from the beer booth, from the food vendors, and from the bands. Sitting outside of it under the shade tree is where my parents, Don and Sue, spend most of the day. This is also where the other members of the Rabbit Hash Historical Society, such as Jane and Carleen, spend most of their time. When people who used to live in the area come to Old Timers Day, they also sit by the museum. It is therefore the spot where today's old timers collect and socialize. The RHHS also raffles off an item donated to them each year in order to raise money for town maintenance. In the past, Louie's mother, Sally Scott, would always make a quilt and donate it to the RHHS to raise money until she passed away in 2007. Others have followed her lead and helped to donate items for the raffle. Besides the raffle, the RHHS also makes money selling other items such as stickers, books, and t-shirts. The most popular items are the DVD's of the movie made about Rabbit Hash along with the posters and postcards advertising the movie, discussed in the

Cindy Schuster sells chances to win a Rabbit Hash wood-burning stove at the very first Old Timers Day. Proceeds went to help build the Rabbit Hash Historical Society Museum. (Photo courtesy of the Clare family)

Rabbit Hash residents (and camera crews) gather for the dedication of the National Register sign on the morning of Old Timers Day, 2004. (Photo courtesy of the Clare family)

next chapter. Throughout the day, many tourists visit the museum, buy items from the RHHS, or donate money. Jane enjoys meeting new people at the museum and talking with them about the town. She finds it very refreshing that people who are not from the Rabbit Hash area have a desire to connect to the town and are just as interested and invested in it, its history, and its wellbeing as those who live in Rabbit Hash.

Next to the museum, Jane's husband sets up his machine that grinds corn into cornmeal. This has not always been part of the Old Timers Day celebration but ties in nicely with the event since it is something old that outsiders enjoy seeing when visiting the town. Jane finds it funny that when she looks over at "that old man grinding cornmeal," it is her husband, just reiterating to her that times have changed and that she is part of the up and coming old timer generation. On the other side of the museum sits the barn. The barn's current function on Old Times Day is the location of the Barnival. A group of locals get together each year and organize games and prizes for children during the day. There is even a performance for the children in the barn with a singer/songwriter who plays fun songs to which the children can sing along and dance. Leslie dresses up as Goofo the clown, conducting games and painting faces.

Across from the barn is the blacksmith shop where the Old Timers Days used to be held. The vendors selling curly fries, burgers,

The barn houses the "Barnival" complete with games and other activities for children on Old Timers Day. (Photo taken by author)

Leslie (aka "Goofo") leads the children's parade on Old Timers Day. (Photo taken by author)

hotdogs, and homemade crafts now set up their operations in this spot. Back across the street and upriver from the barn is the center of the party. This is known as the General Store yard and the music stage, picnic tables, and big tent are located here. This is also where the beer booth is located, right next to the General Store. Soft drinks and water are sold out of a side door of the store and festival t-shirts and lots of other souvenirs are sold inside.

When stepping back and looking at the set up of the town on Old Timers Day, it appears to flow from private history to public party. But both of these are ways for visitors and residents to connect with Rabbit Hash: through a sense of togetherness and festivity or thumbing through old photo albums of the town and past Old Timers Days at the museum. One end of the property provides the public with a glimpse of the private while the other, the actual party, welcomes them in to be a part of the private for at least a day.

Despite the growth of Old Timers Day, the party is still very much organized and run by the Rabbit Hash community. Every year Terrie has a new Old Timers Day t-shirt made each year featuring a different design. She orders many shirts to sell but also has some made up with "Staff" written on the back to give to the locals who work during Old Timers Day. People working in the beer booth, selling soft drinks, taking out garbage, driving the tractor/shuttle, or working in the store

Kenny, one of the shuttle volunteers, transports visitors to and from their cars on Old Timers Day, 2010. (Photo taken by author)

Old Timers Days from Louie Scott's porch. Cornmeal is ground each year on a gristmill next to the museum. (Photo courtesy of Rabbit Hash Historical Society)

receive one of these t-shirts. While they don't cost Terrie too much, they are a wonderful and appreciated way to pay the locals for their help. In fact, this gesture does more than provide those helping with a t-shirt; it gives them a label. The large lettering that reads "Staff" on the back informs everyone who happens to be in town on that day that these people aren't just visiting. The shirt acts as a badge setting those locals apart from the massive amounts of visitors in town. It means that they belong not just on that day, but everyday. Rabbit Hash is more than a one-day event to them; it is their lives. Like everyone in the town, Terrie also admits that she is proud to be a Rabbit Hash local and is more than happy to advertise her role in the community. She says, "I think that people that put forth the effort to make the community should be recognized on that day." This gives the shirt more than material value; it serves as cultural capital. Terrie will not sell these "Staff" shirts to outsiders no matter what price they offer her. I've seen her calmly explain to a pushy customer the day after Old Timers Day that she would not sell him a "Staff" shirt that she had left over no matter what he offered because he had not earned it.

Like many other community events described in folklore works[5] Old Timers Day began as a closed community event but over the years evolved to include the public and has been modified accordingly. Although the locals are still in charge of Old Timers Day, it is really no

Kids play in the hay at Old Timers Day. (Photo taken by author)

Tractor pulls visitors and festival-goers around Old Timers Day (Photo taken by author)

longer for them but for those visiting the event. Even if it is not something that the locals consciously consider, appealing to outside visitors is part of Old Timers Day's goal. Because the town has already been designated as a National Register Historic District, certain expectations must be met. That's where the museum comes in; it acts as a reminder of the past. To spread the word about the town's preservation, every new plaque is unveiled during an Old Timers Day and each new preservation award is mentioned. Every successful event also requires food and drink. Plans are made ahead of time to order more drinks and for certain brands of beer to be included in the beer booth.

Because Old Timers Day is the largest gathering of people in Rabbit Hash throughout the year, it is also a good time for special announcements or remembrances. Each election for mayor, to be discussed at length in the next chapter, has been announced and kicked off at Old Timers Day. When our first mayor, Goofy the dog, passed away, there was a parade and eulogy held in his honor on Old Timers Day. The parade was as long as the town and many locals had a great deal of fun with it by dressing their dogs as people and dressing themselves as dogs. Old Timers Day is one day a year that Rabbit Hash really puts itself on display for the entertainment of outsiders and to celebrate community. It allows the locals to celebrate, demonstrate pride, and show off their community and hard work, and for the visitors it is a day for fun. It is a day for everyone to feel connected, no matter where they are from, because they are all experiencing the day together. Along with this connection between people, there is also a connection to the land and the history of Rabbit Hash. The beautiful scenery, the proximity to the river, the gorgeous sunset, and the old feeling of the town contributes to the allure and explains why it has become one of the most important historic sites in Boone County, Kentucky.

However, as mentioned above, as the event has grown, it no longer seems to be about the community. Instead, the community is most evident the few days before Old Timers Day. The day before is the set up and what many locals consider to be the best part of the event because it is much smaller and only Rabbit Hash locals attend. There are many people with designated jobs such as bringing in the stage, bales of hay, wagons, tables, setting up the tent, and cooking. Everyone knows what is expected of them on this day and all the locals, even if they don't have a designated job, know to show up in town and offer a hand and celebrate their hard work and cooperation. In many ways, the Friday night before Old Timers Day serves the same purpose that Old Timers Day originally did. It is a time that members of the community gather and share food and drink and gossip with a few locals playing music in the background. Many of them have also stressed the importance of that night being just for them and a time to celebrate themselves.

In the interviews I conducted with members of the community that were at the original Old Timers Days, they lament the loss of the Old Timers Days of the past. While everyone admits that tourism is good and necessary for the continued preservation of the town, there is a sense of loss of ownership of what was once so dear to the community. Don admits that the evolution of Old Timers Day was natural but justifies his generation's feeling of loss. "You establish something and then somebody comes along and changes it. You just criticize that." Not only do they feel disconnected to the actual Old Timers Day celebration, but also the night before. It is no longer their generation that spends most of their time in and around the General Store; they have passed the torch.

Because this is an event that has been going on for over thirty years and has shown no signs of slowing down, it has become a valued tradition. In fact, it fits the definition of an invented tradition[6] because it was consciously created, and continues to be recreated, by members of the community to reinforce and legitimate their values of togetherness in a small, historic rural American community. The efforts put forth by Louie and others were to preserve this idea of community that is so commonly associated with old towns, thereby legitimizing this valued aspect of Rabbit Hash as well as the romanticized institution of community. However, this tradition changed as time went on to help fortify other institutions and values. Because Rabbit Hash is a historic district, it is valued within the larger community as a historic jewel. To the tri-state area, Rabbit Hash represents a town that has somehow held onto the traditional old time values of community and the simple life and the community has to accommodate all the people who want to come appreciate it.

Overall, I think that the move from private to public in most of Rabbit Hash's town functions speaks to a sense of loss the nation is experiencing. It is becoming harder and harder to remain connected to the past in America and people everywhere are looking for ways to do that. Rabbit Hash exists as a bridge for individuals in contemporary society to re-connect to a romanticized conception of the past. And even though the events in Rabbit Hash get further and further from the original and authentic small-town experience for the locals, Old Timers Day still serves that purpose for a majority of those in attendance. Although some members of the community do lament the end of the original Old Timers Days, some things haven't changed. It remains a gathering place for the community and serves as reminder and a continuation of what was started by those who came before us.

---

[1] Old Timers Day has been written different ways including "Old Timers' Day" and "Old Timer's Day" and "Old Timers Day". For simplicity, I have chosen to write Old Timers Day, the most commonly seen form.

[2] Santino, Jack, *All Around the Year: Holidays and Celebrations in American Life* (Chicago: University of Illinois Press, 1994), viii.

[3] See Turner, Rory and Phillip H. McArthur, "Cultural Performances: Public Display Events and Festival," in *The Emergence of Folklore in Everyday Life: A Fieldguide and Sourcebook*, ed. George H. Schoemaker (Bloomington: Trickster Press, 1990), 83-93.

[4] See Long, Lucy M. "Apple Butter in Northwest Ohio: Food Festivals and the Construction of Local Meaning," in *Holiday, Ritual, Festival, Celebration, and Public Display*, eds. Cristina Sanchez Carretero and Jack Santino (Spain: Universidad de Alcaia, 2003), 45-65.

[5] See Neustadt, Kathy, *Clambake: A History and Celebration of an American Tradition* (Amherst: University of Massachusetts Press), 1992 as an example.

[6] See Neustadt, *Clambake*, 16 and Hobsbawn, Eric and Terence Ranger, eds., *The Invention of Tradition*, (Cambridge: Cabridge University Press, 1983.)

CHAPTER IV: THE CENTER OF THE UNIVERSE

The attention Rabbit Hash receives manifests itself not only in the form of tourists and traffic. For a period of time, rarely did a week go by in which Rabbit Hash wasn't mentioned in some Greater Cincinnati - Northern Kentucky news program. These segments still occur periodically but Rabbit Hash hasn't been up to many newsworthy antics lately. All of the media attention invading Rabbit Hash reiterates its importance to the greater community. It also causes the Rabbit Hash local community to make adjustments in their persona when cameras are rolling or tourists are present. These adjustments often manifest themselves in the locals' performances that work toward a sense of authenticity.

Authenticity is another concept that stirs debate in many academic circles because it is still unclear what makes something authentic. What is and is not authentic is completely subjective "depend[ing] on who is looking at it, in what context, and for what purpose."[1] However, it is something that is sought after by tourists when traveling to different destinations.[1] According to Regina Bendix:

> The quest for authenticity is a peculiar longing, at once modern and anti-modern. It is oriented toward the recovery of an essence whose loss has been realized only through modernity, and shows recovery is feasible only

through methods and sentiments created in modernity. [1]

Many people visit Rabbit Hash to experience something authentic and old, which includes the preserved buildings and interesting residents. The residents of Rabbit Hash respond to this attention by performing what they feel visitors expect.[1] The audience for the performances (with the well-preserved historic town as their set) is the tourists and the media that come to town. Knowing the expectations of these tourists, the residents of Rabbit Hash negotiate their behavior providing visitors with a "staged authenticity" through their performance.[1] Staged authenticity exists on a continuum between the authentic backstage area, where tourists are not permitted, and the less authentic front area, where the show is performed for them. This suggests that the experience provided for tourists is not necessarily the authentic Rabbit Hash experience but one that is created by the locals and the Rabbit Hash Historical Society.

While the town has been used as the set of a few small films, television shows, and commercials, the performances and staging became a big part of the locals' lives when cameras first starting coming to town to cover the interesting story of Rabbit Hash's name or preservation efforts. The first real Rabbit Hash media craze occurred when Louie put the town up for sale and bought an advertisement in the *National Trust Newspaper*. The fact that an entire town, with a name like Rabbit Hash, was being advertised for sale was a story that many news sources found exceptional and wanted to carry. Don, who Louie put in charge of selling the town, remembers:

> It generated all kinds of publicity. We got calls from all
> over the country, letters…. Morning talk shows would
> call me like Bob and Tom, you know, just to make fun
> and interview me right here on the radio like in L.A. or
> Massachusetts so we got all this free advertising for
> $500…. It was mostly magazine articles and papers.

This attention was nothing compared to what would come to the small town in 1998 and put Rabbit Hash on the map.

Mayor Dogs

The year 1998 marked Boone County, Kentucky's bicentennial and in celebration of this occasion all of the towns in the county were encouraged to hold special events. Rabbit Hash has some very innovative minds and it was decided that an election would be held for Honorary Mayor of Rabbit Hash since it is not an official town with any official local governing powers. In the past, everyone had jokingly referred to Louie as "The Mayor" but it was time to pass the torch. To take this idea one step further, it was decided that this election would be a true mockery of politics and the votes would be based on money. Each vote would cost a dollar and in the end whichever candidate had the most

The Rabbit Hash General Store being transformed for a PBS version of Huckleberry Finn filmed in the town on October 3, 1985.
(Courtesy of Rabbit Hash Historical Society archives and The Kentucky Post)

Goofy, first mayor dog of Rabbit Hash, in his natural position – lounging in the road.
(Donated by Ed Bornamann; Courtesy of the Rabbit Hash Historical Society)

money would be the new mayor. Furthermore, no one was limited to just one vote; everyone could vote as many times as they wanted. Therefore the election was really a fundraiser with all of the money going to the Rabbit Hash Historical Society and its quest to preserve the local East Bend Methodist Church. The election process began normally enough with colorful local people running for office. Eventually, however, some of the local dogs were nominated. Perhaps because it was something of a novelty and because he had some wealthy backers, Goofy, an area mutt, received the most votes making nearly $5,000 for the local church. To be fair to Goofy, he was the most visible candidate in town and spent most of his days in downtown Rabbit Hash. While this was something fun for the Rabbit Hash community to take part in, people outside of the town became fascinated with the dog that became mayor. As a result, the town was on all Cincinnati news programs and in area newspapers. This eventually drew national attention and people began driving to Rabbit Hash, hoping to catch a glimpse of the mayor.

After two years in office, Goofy passed away. He had testicular cancer and had to be put to sleep. Of course the fact that Rabbit Hash euthanized its first elected public official and that his final resting place is rumored to be in a landfill attracted more attention. While outsiders were fascinated, the Rabbit Hash locals put Goofy to rest on Old Timers Day in 2000 with a memorial parade and an official eulogy. The attention culminated in December 2004 with the premiere of a documentary film, *Rabbit Hash: The Center of the Universe*. During the summer of 2002, Jude Prest, director/actor/producer and documentary filmmaker, discovered Rabbit Hash from the Grand Victoria Riverboat Casino across the river in Rising Sun, Indiana. According to Prest, he was working on a Discovery Channel special about riverboat gambling at the Grand Victoria and told the Grand Victoria PR person he wanted to go across the river to film the boat from the opposite shore. She tried to talk him out of it, explaining that it would take over an hour to get there by car and that it was just a strange little town called Rabbit Hash with a dog for mayor. He went anyway and admits that he became obsessed with the story, asking several questions and contacting Terrie at the store who then directed him to Don Clare. Even though his shot of the Grand Victoria, which had some lights out and read "GRA   TORIA," didn't turn out, he was inspired to work on another project. *Rabbit Hash: The Center of the Universe* started out as a project about the election but evolved to incorporate many more aspects of the town including its unique community and charm. Some of the community members were initially skeptical of the film, many others stepped forward and agreed to be interviewed, as Prest discusses:

> I think at first, there was probably a little hesitation. Most
> people got what we were trying to do with the film right
> away... everyone got right behind it. There was one

guy... who absolutely did not want us there... but I think he was just trying to preserve the town's innocence and thought that by us coming in...and doing a movie...that we might ruin the quaintness of the town. Our intent was always to honor and pay homage to the town. But on the whole, everyone was and continues to be amazing!

Prest speaks fondly of his experiences with the town and its locals, and this fondness, to the pleasure and warm reception of the community, is expressed in the film, whose title comes from the fact that so many people in town actually refer to Rabbit Hash as the center of the universe. Prest recalls:

The [review] that always stuck with me the most and was the one I valued the most said that the beauty of the film was that when it starts, you really don't know where I'm going with it. That it looks like I might even be making fun of thes you really start to get that this is an homage. That these are incredible and incredibly smart people....That what e people but that pretty soon into the film, could have been a one joke film really turns out to be a slice of Americana that just doesn't much exist anymore. That one meant an awful lot to me and it was exactly how I structured the film; the idea was to almost

Rabbit Hash: Center of the Universe movie poster.
(Courtesy of the Rabbit Hash Historical Society)

Rabbit Hash: The Center of the Universe producers and crewmembers on the front porch of the
General Store. (Photo courtesy of the Clare family)

make it look like stereotypes at the very beginning and

then turn it all on its ear by showing just how intelligent,

cool and in on the joke the whole town is.

The film fits a trend in the portrayal of rural Americans. These characters are celebrated because of their simplicity and kindness and stand in direct opposition to the more evil, modern, industrialized world.[1] In *The Center of the Universe*, Prest shows that the town of Rabbit Hash has overcome some of the most devastating obstacles for historical locales in the modern world. The people even found a way of getting away from corrupt politicians by voting man's best friend into office. The film also features several individuals that are artists, inventors, and CEO's to counteract some of the more damaging hillbilly stereotypes that abound today in American popular culture.

Of course the film continued to perpetuate the image of

the town as "that town that had a dog for mayor" and

drew more media attention, with Don Clare and Jude

Prest doing television and radio interviews

nearly every day leading up to the premiere of the film. To show their support of the film, the Rabbit Hash locals rented a limousine and went to the Madison Theatre in Covington, Kentucky in style. People from all over the tri-state area came to the premiere because they knew someone who lived in the town or had just been following the

Sue Clare, Louie Scott, and George and Carleen Stephens at the premier of Rabbit Hash: The Center of the Universe at the Madison Theatre in Covington, KY.
(Photo courtesy of the Clare family)

Don Clare being interviewed for Rabbit Hash: The Center of the Universe.
(Photo courtesy of the Clare family)

story. Don and his old friend Danny Wilson played songs inspired by Kentucky and the river, and the Rabbit Hash String Band, which had a band member featured in the film, also performed. It was a very successful night for the film and the theatre, which sold out. Since that time, Jude has taken the film to festivals all over the country, even winning some of them. It is available on DVD and has been a hot-selling item in the General Store and for the Historical Society since its release. It is even available on Netflix.

The popularity of the film speaks to more than simply the election of a dog as mayor; it, along with the number of tourists and strength of the community, speaks to something intangible that Rabbit Hash still possesses despite residing in modern American society. One of the romanticized images in popular culture today is of a small-town community in which everyone knows one another and people live a simple life. Films and television programs feature close-knit groups of friends or neighbors that are not as common in "real life." However, this close community is something that represents old time values and images of what America once was. Rabbit Hash becomes packaged as an authentic old American town where the old-fashioned values of community and simplicity have remained intact despite the evolution of the rest of the society. Rabbit Hash becomes more than just the physical town but rather a bridge to the romanticized American past, a way to

The 2004 Mayoral Election "Rules" are explained at the launch of the election during Old Timers Day. (Donated by Louie Scott; Courtesy of the Rabbit Hash Historical Society)

Junior Cochran is announced the winner of the 2004 Mayoral Election. (Photo courtesy of the Clare family)

remain connected to the land, the country, and its history. While this was not Jude's admitted intention, his film serves the same purpose as other popular culture texts with similar themes. However, the documentary nature of the film gives it a sense of authenticity because the people and events featured in it are all true, but with certain details carefully left out.

Because of all of the attention the film received, Don Clare announced at Old Timers Day 2004 that the mourning period for Goofy was over and the polls were open to determine the next honorary mayor. To get things rolling, Don nominated his own family pets, Lu-Lu the pot-bellied pig and Higgins the miniature donkey, to kick off the election. Votes were cast for both of them along with a turtle in attendance, a few of the local dogs, and the cat that protected the General Store from mice. From the start of this election, no human even had a chance. This brought much more media attention to the town from local sources, national sources, and eventually international sources.

Everyone knew that the attention surrounding this election was going to be significant but the level it actually reached was unfathomable. Because the presidential election of 2004 was very serious, the humor of the Rabbit Hash election was a nice break for the media covering the national election. The first hint of the stories catchiness was when Don was featured on ESPN's top ten weird stories for the day. After that CNN jumped in and did a story in which they met with several of the candidates

Jane Cochran and her dog Junior being interviewed about Junior's term as Mayor of Rabbit Hash. (Photo courtesy of Jane Cochran)

Junior
Mayor of Rabbit Hash, KY

Postcard sold by the RHHS featuring Junior in front of the General Store. (Courtesy of the Rabbit Hash Historical Society)

and talked to several of the locals. The host from CNN put himself in the running, but throughout the entire segment, the only vote he had was his own. The attention culminated with a call from *Jimmy Kimmel Live* which did a live satellite interview with the candidates and their owners on the evening of Monday, October 18, 2004. The town was literally buzzing that night with the sound of the satellite truck emanating throughout town. The owners of the candidates led them all into the General Store one by one. The candidates didn't know exactly what was happening to them, but they enjoyed sniffing one another. Most of them were quite easy to manage but the pig and donkey were a different story. Poor Lu-Lu screamed the entire time and Higgins took advantage of the new location and relieved himself on the front porch. The interview was successful and that night, after Monday night football, the news, and *Nightline*, Rabbit Hash made its late-night television debut.

On November 2, 2004, after voting for the national election in the basement of the Iron Works, locals began collecting in the barn across the street to hear the results of the Rabbit Hash mayoral election. It was tense at first while the biggest supporters of each of the candidates debated on how many more "votes" they should cast for their candidate. In the end, Junior, a black lab owned by Jane Burch Cochran and her husband, was announced mayor. A proud Jane boasted, "I sleep with the mayor."

2008 Mayoral election posters hanging on the door of the barn. (Donated by Louie Scott; Courtesy of the Rabbit Hash Historical Society)

A crowd gathers around the stage to listen to bands and the candidates' election speeches at the 2008 Rabbit Hash Mayoral Election Rally. (Photo taken by author)

With Junior came even more publicity. He was a guest on a morning talk show following his election and was a part of many Cincinnati activities. Junior's powerful position was even featured in a special on *Animal Planet*, also made, produced, and directed by Jude Prest and *The Center of the Universe* crew. *Mayor Dog* followed Junior on his campaign trail, showing what he did around his community to help out. *Animal Planet* required a charity aspect of the program so Junior was shown breaking ground for a Boone County dog park and as the spokes-dog for the Women's Crisis Center of Northern Kentucky. Women are often hesitant to leave abusive environments because they fear for their pets. This particular shelter offers women a place for their pets as well so that they too will be safe from abuse. While there is no doubt that *Mayor Dog* was well-done, it failed to capture the Rabbit Hash feel like the previous film. There were paid actors in the special along with helicopter footage, a tour bus, makeup and hair stylists, and narration by Ben Stein.

After *Mayor Dog*, the craze began to die and Rabbit Hash began to settle back down and out of the public eye. However, tragedy struck in May of 2008 when Junior passed away. At Old Timers Day 2008, a new election began. Higgins returned and had a good showing but the dogs definitely represented the majority of the candidates. In October, a day-long political rally was held in downtown. Each of the candidates were invited to "speak" and several bands played. Of course, there was also the

Don Clare and the 2008 Mayoral candidates dedicate the new, state-of-the-art outhouse in Rabbit Hash. (Photo taken by author)

Pike, 2008 Mayoral candidate, rests at his table at the rally. (Photo taken by author)

opportunity to vote. It was a wonderfully successful day despite the heated debates.

This election, like the 2004 Rabbit Hash election, received a great deal of national attention with candidates campaigning with the help of news cameras and radio interviews on almost a daily basis. Historical Society board member Bob Schrage speaks fondly of the time he spent campaigning with his 170 pound St. Bernard and Shepherd mix family member, Rembrandt, who was even asked to make appearances at local businesses, made several television appearances, and was featured in many newspaper articles. The national appeal of this election had checks being mailed to the Rabbit Hash Historical Society in the name of a particular candidate. In fact, a mysterious check and letter from a Barry O. in Chicago came in support of Higgins which had everyone wondering if the 2008 presidential candidates were following our election. And more votes were also cast online at the Rabbit Hash Historical Society's website using PayPal.

This national attention culminated on CBS's *Sunday Morning* with Bill Geist. Cameras were in attendance at the Rabbit Hash political rally and Mr. Geist spent some time interviewing and walking candidates. Like the 2004 election, the 2008 election was so widely received by the national media and spoke to many frustrated Americans who had reached their limit of political debates, campaigns, slander, and pettiness. The mockery

Bobbi delivers Lucy Lou's speech on her behalf at the 2008 rally. (Photo taken by author)

Bob Schrage with his dog, Rembrandt, who ran for Mayor in the 2008 election. (Photo courtesy of Bob Schrage)

of the election taking place in Rabbit Hash was a relief from the seriousness of the national election and the desperation and hopelessness felt by many who felt their needs weren't being met.

The results were once again announced on election night in the Rabbit Hash barn. It was a jovial time away from the worry and anticipation surrounding the national election. In the end, Lucy Lou, a young border collie, was named mayor of Rabbit Hash. Since taking her post, she has been the most active mayor: she is in downtown Rabbit Hash every weekday with Bobbi, her owner, and takes her position seriously as welcoming committee seriously. She offers everyone a stick as a souvenir of their visit and if that stick is thrown, she gladly runs after it making sure to bring it right back. She and Bobbi have also been featured on many local news programs promoting town functions and most recently she received a check on behalf of the Rabbit Hash Historical Society from *Reader's Digest*. With the town in Lucy Lou's capable paws, no new election is in sight.

Constructing an Image

While it is indisputable that Rabbit Hash has been influenced by the media, the town and its community members do their fair share of perpetuating its small-town image and values. There are several products that are created for and sold in the General Store that work to do this,

Lucy Lou, third dog mayor of Rabbit Hash, is in town regularly greeting visitors and locals.
(Photo by Steph Keller; Courtesy of Bobbi Kayser)

A member of the Reader's Digest team passes out treats to Mayor Lucy Lou and her friends.
(Photo courtesy of the Clare family)

along with many informational pamphlets and websites created by the Rabbit Hash community for the benefit and pleasure of visitors.[1] For many of the newer visitors to town, their first impression of Rabbit Hash is not when they first drive through or step into the town. Rather, they've come into contact with the image of the General Store which has been reproduced in the form of postcards, paintings, television footage, pictures in newspapers or magazines, and on the internet. Therefore, the visitors' first experiences with Rabbit Hash are mediated and that fully informs and affects how they will experience the town while visiting. Yet through these mediated sources, the Rabbit Hash community has a hand in the construction of the image.

Once in the town, and especially inside the General Store, the image-production continues with the products being sold. The most popular items are beverages. This is often a beer but most likely a soda, of which the General Store offers a diverse array. Many of them are organic but others simply represent the past. While Coca-Cola can be purchased in the regular twenty-ounce bottles, it can also be purchased in the eight-ounce glass bottles, which, as discussed previously in the first chapter, helps to serve as a bridge to another time, a simple past previously constructed by Coca-Cola's image. Other than the old Coke bottles, old-fashioned root beer and sarsaparilla are sold. These are also hard-to-find items that have an old-time feel. Ale-8-One is another popular soda sold

The original Rabbit Hash Iron Works t-shirt. This design is still printed on t-shirts and sold in the General Store today. (Photo courtesy of author)

in the General Store since it is made in Kentucky.

Other than drinks and snacks, the best selling items in the General Store say Rabbit Hash on them somewhere. The first items to sell-out are always the t-shirts. Many of the t-shirts have the image of the General Store on them with "Rabbit Hash General Store" written above it. There are also t-shirts with Herb the hillbilly on them. I have a difficult time looking at these objectively because they are images to which I have grown quite accustomed. It also took me many years to find the humor in the "Volunteer Fire Department, String Band, and SWAT Team" shirts as well as the Rabbit Hash Iron Works shirts that advertise "Tomcats Thrashed" and "Widows Tended" as some of the jobs they perform. When I remove myself from the perspective of a local who has grown up on these images, the content of the shirts becomes much funnier.

I have always said that growing up in Rabbit Hash makes nothing seem weird. In many ways, as a child, you just accept things for what they are and have no comparison to the way things really are in other parts of the world. It took me getting out in the world to actually look at my hometown and realize that there is something weird going on there and that the people in the town do have an amazing sense of humor about it all. The Herb t-shirts perpetuate the hillbilly stereotype that many people seem to have about Rabbit Hash and the surrounding areas – as a place in the middle of nowhere Kentucky where people aren't fully aware of how civilized society works. The String Band t-shirts speak to the small-town aspect of Rabbit Hash by suggesting that as a member of the community, you are needed to fulfill all of these necessary tasks. In fact it is stated in the film that all you need to do to be a part of it all is to buy a t-shirt. The Iron Works t-shirt serves a similar function by including obscure tasks as under the job requirement of an Iron Works employee. The humor in these t-shirts and the Rabbit Hash name stand out to visitors and tourists as well as passersby who may see the shirts when they are worn. The image of the store and of Herb the hillbilly also grace ceramic mugs, can coozies, magnets, patches, stickers, and hats and all serve the same purpose as the t-shirts; they are keepsakes of a visit to the small Kentucky town that bring the owner closer to history and old-time values. In some circles, the t-shirts act as cultural capital. I wear my old Rabbit Hash t-shirts that have been passed down to me from my parents with pride. It seems, that since my t-shirts are older, they are therefore closer to the beginning, the authentic Rabbit Hash experience.

Postcards are also a top seller in the store because they sit close to the register and are much cheaper than the other items for sale. The most popular postcard of the General Store is a photograph that was taken in the 1980's. In front of the General Store, instead of a slew of motorcycles, is a horse drawn wagon. There are also people sitting on the porch of the store in bib overalls and long dresses. This is, in all actuality, a picture postcard image of small-town USA where time is seemingly standing still. While this was a day that actually occurred in the town and was not setup for the sole purpose of creating this particular image, the fact that this image was chosen to represent the General Store to be sold to visitors is an act by the town and General Store operator to construct an old and historic feel of Rabbit Hash for visitors to take home with them.

Most of the other postcards feature the highly recognizable outside of the General Store, but the store is not the focal point. In one particular postcard, the fuzzy background of the postcard is the General Store and the focal point is a row of motorcycles parked out front. This image is very different from the image in the last postcard discussed because it is not attempting to sell Rabbit Hash as a historic town where time stands still but rather it functions as a souvenir for those who visit Rabbit Hash solely because of its status as a necessary stop for area bikers. Other items in the store have catered to this particular group of Rabbit Hash visitors such as patches and pins for bikers' leathers and stickers to go on the bike itself.

Another popular postcard features an old photo of three teenage boys lounging on the ground. Each of them has what can only be described as a "shit-eating" grin, looking as if they have been caught, with two rifles, a pistol, a knife, and a bottle of liquor. This photograph is said

Postcard of the Stephen's General Store in Rabbit Hash. (Photo courtesy of the Clare family)

Postcard sold by the Rabbit Hash Historical Society commemorating the 175th anniversary of the Rabbit Hash General Store. (Photo courtesy of the Rabbit Hash Historical Society)

to have been found in the General Store but no information, like the names of the boys and the year, are given. It is assumed that these were local boys who were participating in good ole boy activities like shooting and drinking and conjures up feelings of a simpler life when carrying guns and underage drinking weren't social problems, just a way of life. These boys also could be the inspiration behind Herb, the lounging hillbilly discussed earlier. Either way, this postcard image still sells a stereotypical aspect of Rabbit Hash's culture even though the General Store is not present in the photo.

The most recent postcard is of Lucy Lou with an American flag background, her name, and her paw print signature. When Junior became mayor, there was a postcard of him wearing his red, white, and blue hat and a bow tie in front of the General Store. Junior's image also graced thelabels of hot sauces, spices, and herbs such as the popular Hillbilly Butt Rub. Therefore, Junior became another representative image of Rabbit Hash based more on the media attention and tourism than on history. Lucy Lou is continuing this tradition with her postcard and her photo on the labels of her own Mayor Select line of wine sold in the wine store in the Iron Works.

Another way that Rabbit Hash works to shape its own image is through the internet. There are two major websites dedicated to the town along with various MySpace and facebook pages. The first website is

RabbitHash.com and is the site for the Rabbit Hash General Store. The website's homepage is a brown scale of several children sitting on the front porch of the General Store. Every time a new page on the website loads, a different saying "going round town" such as, "Pert near, but not plumb," and "Work? That's for donkeys and they turn their ass up at it," appears. However, they all speak to the old country aspects of the town as well as perpetuate the country stereotype. This is also demonstrated on the menu where certain things are spelled phonetically like "tell yer friends," "how to git here," and "give us a holler." The website provides dates of all the activities going on in town as well as valuable information including directions and some history. The most interesting aspect of the website is that people are able to join and leave comments. In the history section of the website, several people have posted questions about the history, attempting to tie themselves to the town through ancestors and even acquaintances. This desire to remain connected to Rabbit Hash became most evident to me while working in the store when visitors would tell me about how they had a grandmother or great uncle who lived in Rabbit Hash or visited the town years ago. As described previously, this is an extension of the desire that many of us have to remain connected to a piece of American history that is seemingly unchanged by time. We can do this through purchasing souvenirs, visits to the town, and even tracing our genealogy to the town's earlier years.

The second website is run by the Rabbit Hash Historical Society, RabbitHashUSA.com. This site also attempts the country feel. The background resembles old boards like those from a barn and the menu is on a spiral-bound notebook with a font that looks like handwriting. The menu also says things like "happenins," "tobacco," "notions," and "potions" that link to pages about the history, the mayor, or the Rabbit Hash Historical Society. The construction of the website also speaks to an old rustic simplicity as does the terminology of the menu. Because it is run by the RHHS and not the General Store, the interests are a bit different. Rather than a calendar of events, this website offers a more detailed history of Rabbit Hash and information about the RHHS and its goals. Because the mayor is affiliated more with the RHHS, having raised many funds for the non-profit organization, there is a portion dedicated to Lucy Lou, Junior, Goofy, and election results. Overall, it sells the same image of Rabbit Hash as the previous webpage but focuses more on the organization and the mayor rather than the General Store's emphasis on products and community.

The Friends of Rabbit Hash General Store on MySpace was the first social networking page for Rabbit Hash. It started out mostly as a way for local bands to connect with Terrie about performing in Rabbit Hash. The Rabbit Hash General Store's Sundays Behind the Stove (during the winter months) and the barn dances during the summer have become

highly sought-after gigs for bands from all over the Greater Cincinnati -
Northern Kentucky area. Bobbi Kayser maintains the MySpace page,
keeping the few locals that are on MySpace in the top friends along with
the bands that are playing in Rabbit Hash in the near future or have
played in the recent past. Bobbi has been a big part of the music in Rabbit
Hash, making fliers for the events as well as getting many of the bands to
contact Terrie about playing in town. She feels that Rabbit Hash is
coveted by so many area bands because, unlike in bars, they are able to
maintain a connection to the crowd because of the closeness of the
setting. It also allows for outsiders to become part of the Rabbit Hash
community. People follow the bands to Rabbit Hash and contribute to
the potluck. By sharing a dish and the experience with one another,
tourists are more likely to relate to the locals. This can create a somewhat
nostalgic feeling making them excited that they are so warmly received by
'those nice country folk.'

Terrie, Bobbi, Don, Lucy Lou, and many others also have
facebook pages that advertise activities going on in Rabbit Hash. Each
week, many people upload photographs and videos of their time in the
town. Many also upload their photos to two different facebook groups:
the Rabbit Hash group and the Rabbit Hash Friends group. Everyone
posting on these pages share a love for the town and their experiences
there. These pages serve as another way for individuals who cannot

experience the town on a daily basis to remain connected to it. The pages also work to legitimize one's relationship with the town by providing a space for people to share that they grew up in the area or knew someone who did, have traveled there often, or know a piece of its history.

All of these websites have a positive impact on the town by advertising its events and spreading its merits and appeal. However, they pale in comparison to an actual visit to the town.

<u>Performing Rabbit Hash</u>

While the locals are proud of their town and are happy to share it with outsiders and visitors, they also admit to performing or putting on a show for the visitors. While these tactics are not meant to scare off the outsiders, they serve as a reminder that this is their community and that when the visitors leave, the locals will still be there. Again, I feel this speaks to the pride that the Rabbit Hash locals have for their town and it takes some testing of the outsiders to make sure that they are willing to respect the town for what it is, including the people in it. While some of the Rabbit Hash locals, including myself, are concerned with our public image and whether or not the media is going to shape the Rabbit Hash community as a bunch of backward hillbillies, most people are not. However, some of them do admit to performing certain roles and acting out certain stereotypes when outsiders are around. This is sometimes a test and sometimes for their own amusement. Tommy is one local who exemplifies this characteristic; he is friendly to everyone but always out to make someone laugh. If this requires that he play the hillbilly, then he will. He refers to it as "Put[ting] on a little hillbilly charm." He says, "If they're all nice and polite and need a hand or something, we put on the southern gentlemen charm type thing... but if they roll in here and they're all rude and pompous and uppity we turn on the redneck thing." There seems to be a clear distinction to Tommy between the hillbilly and the redneck. The hillbilly is the friendly country person, while the redneck represents the more negative image given to country people.[1]

This first became apparent to me with my first viewing of *Rabbit Hash: The Center of the Universe*. Initially, some people were concerned that the producers of the film would cast Rabbit Hash and its residents in a negative light. However, as mentioned before, Jude and his co-workers meant to highlight the charm and positive aspects of the, admittedly, strange residents. For the most part, after finally seeing the film, locals and participants in the documentary were quite pleased and found the film to be accurate to their lives and their stories. However, some outsiders that I have talked to that have seen the film have been uncomfortable with the ways in which certain individuals conform to what they consider negative rural stereotypes. In the film, those interviewed were chosen because they fell into one of two different categories: those that conformed to popular rural stereotypes and those who stood in opposition to them. Those that conform to the stereotypes were chosen because of the dress (such as bib overalls), their long beards, the way they spoke, the stories they told, and the instruments they played. Others such as authors, architects, artists, CEO's, and professors blow these stereotypes. And some of those interviewed straddled both categories appearing, or acting, as hillbillies but in their personal lives are renowned doctors and respected local historians. They put on a show for the cameras by purposefully conforming to stereotypes and then negating these with their merits.

As Tommy mentioned above, other locals admit to putting on these types of performances not only for cameras but for visitors. Terrie Markesbery admits to performing certain stereotypes or acting a certain way when outsiders come to town:

> Let's keep it quirky kind of thing. I do sort of go by that because, you know, it's Rabbit Hash. I've said that to people before, "Well, it's Rabbit Hash. You don't expect me to hurry or give you good service do you because I don't want you to get used to that…." Everything can be a little crooked or everything can be just slightly off because we somehow have a little bit of leeway there.

This is something that Terrie suggests sets us apart from the visitors. She says:

I think that they're stereotyping because they don't

expect to see that when they come in, that you're hip to

the scene. I think they expect that we're out of touch or

backwards and you know we're not ... so sometimes it's

fun to play on that. Yeah, I definitely play with it.

Many have suggested that the outsiders sometimes harm the locals,

whether consciously or not, by expecting them to conform to certain

stereotypes of country people. These stereotypes fit both categories of

redneck and hillbilly. In order to protect themselves from these

stereotypes that suggest exploitation and a struggle for power, the Rabbit

Hash locals consciously enact the stereotypes, thereby giving them control

of the situation. If, for some reason, the local does not feel like playing on

a certain day, the visitors of Rabbit Hash may not walk away with the

authentic experience they were expecting. This further reinforces the

binary of us vs. them, country vs. city, simplicity vs. fast-paced life, and it

all falls under the control of the Rabbit Hash local.

Terrie also discusses how some of the stereotypes she performs

aren't necessarily a conscious effort, but because they make sense and fit

the lifestyle that Rabbit Hash necessitates:

Playing a little bit, I do.... I sometimes feel like I'm

fitting this stereotype when I bring wood in, or carrying a

pail of water or something because it sort of feels like

that's what women back in the day would be doing....
Wearing hiking boots with a skirt because it's practical
and because you need to.... I've seen so many high-
heeled women get stuck in those crevices.

However, there is also a point in which one must succumb to the
possibility that some stereotypes exist for a reason. Living a rustic lifestyle
does necessitate certain activities that are stereotypical of a hillbilly or
redneck life. This matter-of-fact way of looking at stereotypes was
broached during just one of my interviews when the interviewee
mentioned that there are actual hillbillies in the area who dress, talk, and
live in a way that conforms to stereotypical images. Yet many people who
do so do it purposefully to exercise power and control over outsiders.
When around only community members, locals are themselves. This may
include actions that fit under certain stereotypes. However, when
outsiders are present, the locals are aware they are being observed and
those same actions then become a performance. It is the locals' awareness
of the outsider that makes the action a performance. If the locals were
completely oblivious to how they may appear to outsiders, then the
outsiders would have the power and could stereotype accordingly. It is the
knowledge of the possibility of stereotyping that gives the local the power
in this particular situation. This is not simply one-sided either. The locals
are also quick to stereotype outsiders when they enter the town and can

change their act accordingly, as previously suggested by Tommy.

Eventually these performances have become second nature because of repetition.[1] Don Clare is a good example of this. His wife, Sue, discusses how he has changed the way he talks since moving to Rabbit Hash. He now uses improper grammar and pronunciations that used to irritate him; long A's and wrong uses of verbs such as, "I seen it." Sue says that it "was conscious at first" and "made him look the part" but now it has infiltrated his regular speech patterns.

Rabbit Hash, according to Bob Schrage, is the kind of place that always elicits a positive and excited response when mentioned, and every year, more and more people visit the town of Rabbit Hash after first seeing it on television or hearing about it through word of mouth. This constant increase in tourism creates a demand for souvenirs and information that perpetuate the town's authentic historic country image. The locals then become responsible for the feelings the tourists leave with, having created all of the products and information themselves. The locals also perform for the visitors to contribute to the authenticity and feel of the town. However, the experience each individual leaves with is dependent upon their own attitudes and their desire to connect to the town and its history.

[1] Evans-Pritchard, Deirdre, "The Portal Case: Authenticity, Tourism, Traditions, and the Law" in *Folk Groups and Folklore Genres: A Reader*, ed. Elliot Oring (Logan: Utah State University Press, 1989), 49.

[2] See Evans-Pritchard, "The Portal Case," 43-51 and Molz, Jennie Germann, "Tasting an Imagined Thailand: Authenticity and Culinary Tourism in Thai Restaurants" in *Culinary Tourism*, ed. Lucy M. Long (Lexington: The University Press of Kentucky, 2004), 53-75.

[3] Bendix, Regina, *In Search of Authenticity: The Formation of Folklore Studies* (Madison: University of Wisconsin Press, 1997), 8.

[4] For information on performance theory in the field of folklore, see Bauman, Richard, *Verbal Art as Performance* (Rowley, MA: Newbury House Publishers, 1977) and Paredes, Americo and Richard Bauman, eds., *Toward New Perspectives in Folklore* (Bloomington: Trickster Press, 2000).

[5] For a discussion of staged authenticity, see MacCannel, Dean, *The Tourist: A New Theory of the Leisure Class* (Los Angeles: University of California Press, 1999) and Molz, "Tasting an Imagined Thailand."

[6] Harkins, Anthony, *Hillbilly: A Cultural History of an American Icon* (New York: Oxford University Press, 2004), 162.

[7] See Dorst, John D., *The Written Suburb: An American Site, An Ethnographic Dilemma* (Philadelphia: University of Pennsylvania Press, 1989) for a post-modern ethnographic discussion about how the town of Chadd's Ford, PA presents itself through printed materials.

[8] See Price, Angeline F., "Working Class Whites" in *Signs of Life in the USA: Readings on Popular Culture for Writers*, Eds. Sonia Maasik and Jack Solomon, 5th ed. (Boston: Bedford/St. Martin's, 2006), 591-596 for further discussion of this dichotomy.

[9] Hamera, Judith, ed., *Opening Acts: Performance in/as Communication and Cultural Studies* (Thousand Oaks, CA: Sage Publications, 2006), 6.

CONCLUSION

The work that I have done on Rabbit Hash has been a life-long project. My research really began as observations I made when I was working in the Rabbit Hash General Store and started to recognize how the town appealed to many different types of people. This experience renewed my love for the town, something that I had lost while in high school. Finding an outlet for my interest in the work of many cultural theorists, anthropologists, and folklorists helped to shape the project into what it is.

Throughout this study, I look at the perceived history of Rabbit Hash and how it has shaped the lives of community members and the experiences of visitors and the media. Rabbit Hash serves as a reminder of the idealized American past that stressed the importance of a simple life and traditional values. Rabbit Hash is a bridge to that past and speaks to those who feel a sense of loss of traditional America and traditional values. The preservation effort put forth by those living in the town and how they choose to live their lives is a way for them to remain connected to the past. Because history and tradition are concepts shaped and molded by the people, the connection that the residents maintain is a feeling of ownership. While they do not actually own it, the most popular stories that circulate through town focus on the people that were there before.

The most popular story about the name's origin gives credit to someone living in the town. Therefore the residents are self-sustaining and don't require anything from outsiders.

Central to shaping Rabbit Hash into an idealized American small town is the sense of community. The importance of community is stressed by everyone living in the town. The locals make their presence known and strive to work together in the best interest of preserving the town's rich history. Community events and the breaking of bread make everyone an equal. The locals of Rabbit Hash exhibit communitas in these events, especially in the liminoid space of weekends in the town when work-week lives are forgotten and time is suspended in the rural setting of Rabbit Hash. Community is also something that is achieved actively. The residents of Rabbit Hash actively and intentionally work to achieve the sense of community and continually define themselves by emphasizing what they are not: a constructed subdivision community. This allows them the opportunity to expand their circle to include interesting individuals that don't necessarily fit in elsewhere and the freedom to make themselves stand apart from regular society. This unique community is something that keeps the residents around and draws in new people.

The importance of community is stressed in the annual Old Timers Day celebration held in Rabbit Hash over Labor Day weekend. This celebration marks a transition from the private to the public realm.

What was once a very private event, shared by only the members of the Rabbit Hash community, has become more and more popular over the years and is now open to the public, even advertised. Today, Old Timers Day is a time when the Rabbit Hash community comes together to share their town with many outside visitors. There is an effort made on the part of all of the volunteers to give the visitors an authentic Rabbit Hash experience by offering food, drink, and old-time music. This conception of authenticity is based on what the Rabbit Hash residents think the tourists want and expect from an event with a name like "Old Timers Day." Because the celebration is an invented tradition that changes with each generation, there are different ideas of what the day should be. The newer crowd enjoys the party and catering to visitors while the older residents who have participated in Old Timers Day from the very beginning lament the days when it was just about them and preserving the town and community.

Another way in which Rabbit Hash has been made public is through its growing popularity in many different forms of media. Rabbit Hash has become a popular music venue and tourist site. This popularity is due to the media attention surrounding Rabbit Hash's tumultuous political history and the movie and news stories about it. In many ways, members of the Rabbit Hash community shape the town themselves by performing for outsiders and the cameras, creating the image being sold to the public by the news media and in the General Store. The websites dedicated to Rabbit Hash provide a perfect opportunity to shape the image of the town presented to outsiders. Rabbit Hash is most often perceived as a backwards rural town fostering hillbillies with bad grammar. Many of the locals admit to performing that role when outsiders are around to help distinguish themselves from visitors and to maintain some power over them. This performance is not a performance in the traditional theatrical sense because there is no stage or backstage. Instead, Rabbit Hash has only a middle ground where the locals must constantly negotiate what they think visitors expect and what they themselves do in their daily lives.

What exactly is it that makes Rabbit Hash so popular? What I can deduce from my observations, interviews, and reading is that Rabbit Hash speaks to a wide variety of people because of the values placed on historic sites in this country today. Rabbit Hash serves as a bridge to the past and by visiting or tracing connections to the town and the buildings in it, one is able to connect oneself to America and therefore have a tie to the land. The work that the community has done to preserve the town has become a source of pride for the residents and something that visitors and outsiders admire. The stress placed on community by the residents is a self-perpetuated cycle. People move to the area for the small town community and work to maintain it. With the concerted efforts of everyone who is affected by time spent in Rabbit Hash, it can be guaranteed that the town will remain as it is for future generations to experience and use in the same ways.

In the end, I have learned a great deal about my town and the people in it. I have a new-found respect for Rabbit Hash and all of the residents and greatly appreciate and value my experiences there. I hope that my work has helped the town by spreading the word about the efforts made to preserve it and to encourage others to visit and share the unique Rabbit Hash experience with us. When starting this project, I was warned there is the danger of romanticizing this town because of my closeness to it. While I tried to be critical in my analysis, I also cannot help but think that yes, my town is all that it is cracked up to be. It is a great place to call my home and full of people that I love and depend on. It's accepting atmosphere creates an environment that people long to be a part of, and that is why I think that Rabbit Hash is so popular and will continue to survive long into the future. It gives me hope that some parts of America are not completely obsessed with the new and modern but do have a deep respect for history and maintaining an invaluable connection to it.

BIBLIOGRAPHY

Baudrillard, Jean. *The System of Objects*. 1996. Trans. James Benedict. New York: Verso, 2005.

Bauman, Richard. "Performance." *Folklore, Cultural Performances, and Popular Entertainments*. Ed. Richard Bauman. New York: Oxford University Press, 1992. 41-49.
---. *Verbal Art as Performance*. Rowley, MA: Newbury House Publishers, 1977.

Bendix, Regina. *In Search of Authenticity: The Formation of Folklore Studies*. Madison: University of Wisconsin Press, 1997.

Bob. Personal interview. January 7, 2007.

Brown, Linda Keller, and Kay Mussell, eds. *Ethnic and Regional Foodways in the United States: The Performance of Group Identity*. Knoxville,TN: University of Tennessee Press, 1984.

Burrison, John. *Roots of a Region: Southern Folk Culture*. Jackson, Miss.: University of Mississippi Press, 2007.

Byrne, Pat. "Booze, Ritual, and the Invention of Tradition: The Phenomenon of the Newfoundland Screech-In." *Usable Pasts: Traditions and Group Expressions in North America*. Ed. Tad Tuleja. Logan, UT: Utah State University Press, 1997. 232- 248.

Clare, Callie, Caitlyn Clare, and Donald Clare, Jr. "The History of Rabbit Hash." *Ancestry: Our Ohio River Heritage*. Mt. Vernon, IN: Windmill Publications, Inc., 1996. 24-66.

Clare, Callie. *Boone County Recorder*. October, 2004.

Clare, Don, Jr. Personal interview. January 23, 2006.

Clare, Sue. Personal interview. January 15, 2007.

Cochran, Jane Burch. Personal interview. November 24, 2006.

Dorst, John D. *The Written Suburb: An American Site, An Ethnographic*

Dilemma. Philadelphia: University of Pennsylvania Press, 1989.

Doyle, Duane. Personal interview. January 6, 2007.

Eliason, Eric A. "Pioneers and Recapitulation in Mormon Popular Historical Expression." *Usable Pasts: Traditions and Group Expressions in North America.* Ed. Tad Tuleja. Logan, UT: Utah State University Press, 1997. 175-211.

Evans-Pritchard, Deirdre. "The Portal Case: Authenticity, Tourism, Traditions, and the Law." *Folk Groups and Folklore Genres: A Reader.* Ed. Elliot Oring. Logan, UT: Utah State University Press, 1989. 43-51.

Feintuch, Burt. "Longing for Community." *Western Folklore* 60 (2001): 149-161.

Friends of Rabbit Hash General Store Myspace Page. February 28, 2011 <http://profile.myspace.com/index.cfm?fuseaction=user.viewpr ofile&friendid=58068773&MyToken=a7bf416f-a301-4327-b005-80a8f5e1030b>.

Geertz, Clifford. "Deep Play: Notes on the Balinese Cockfight." *The Interpretation of Cultures.* New York: Basic Books, Inc., 1973. 412-453.
---. "Thick Description: Toward an Interpretive Theory of Culture." *The Interpretation of Cultures.* New York: Basic Books, Inc., 1973. 3-30.

Gladstone, Gary. *Reaching Climax and Other Towns Along the American Highway: More Portraits from the Heartland.* Berkeley: Ten Speed Press, 2006.

Glassie, Henry. *Material Culture.* Bloomington: Indiana University Press, 1999.
---. "The Appalachian Log Cabin. *Baseball, Barns, and Bluegrass: A Geography of American Folklife.* Ed. George O. Carnery. New York: Rowman and Littlefield Publishers, Inc., 1998. 19-28.
---. *The Stars of Ballymenone.* Bloomington, IN: Indiana University Press, 2006.
---. "Tradition." *Eight Words for the Study of Expressive Culture.* Ed. Burt Feintuch. Chicago: University of Illinois Press, 2003. 176-197.

Green, Leslie. Personal interview. December 30, 2006.

Gusfield, Joseph R. "The Social Meaning of Meals: Hierarchy and Equality in the American Pot-Luck." *Contemporary Studies in Sociology (Volume 12) Self, Collective Behavior and Society: Essays Honoring the Contributions of Ralph H. Turner. Ed. Gerald M. Platt and Chad Gordon*. Greenwich, CT: Jai Press Inc., 1994.

Hamera, Judith, ed. *Opening Acts: Performance in/ as Communication and Cultural Studies*. Thousand Oaks, CA: Sage Publications, 2006.

Handler, Richard and Jocelyn Linnekin. "Tradition, Genuine or Spurious." *Folk Groups and Folklore Genres: A Reader*. Ed. Elliot Oring. Logan, UT: Utah State University Press, 1989. 38-42.

Harkins, Anthony. *Hillbilly: A Cultural History of an American Icon*. New York: Oxford University Press, 2004.

Kamau, Lucy Jayne. "Liminality, Communitas, Charisma, and Community." *Intentional Community: An Anthropological Perspective*. Ed. Susan Love Brown. Albany, NY: State University of New York Press, 2002. 17-40.

Kapchan, Deborah A. "Performance." *Eight Words for the Study of Expressive Culture*. Ed. Burt Feintuch. Chicago: University of Illinois Press, 2003. 176-197.

Kayser, Bobbi. Personal interview. November 25, 2006.

Lents, R.V., et al. *Now and Then*. Walton, KY: Walton Advertiser, 1977.

Long, Lucy M. "Apple Butter in Northwest Ohio: Food Festivals and the Construction of Local Meaning." *Holiday, Ritual, Festival, Celebration, and Public Display*. Eds. Cristina Sanchez Carretero and Jack Santino. Spain: Universidad de Alcaia, 2003. 45-65.

MacCannell, Dean. *The Tourist: A New Theory of the Leisure Class*. Los Angeles: University of California Press, 1999.

Markesbery, Terrie. Personal interview. November 27, 2006.

McCracken, Grant. "The Evocative Power of Things: Consumer Goods and the Preservation of Hopes and Ideals." *Culture and Consumption: New Approaches to the Symbolic Character of Consumer Goods and Activities*. Bloomington, IN: Indiana University Press,

1988. 104-117.

Molz, Jennie Germann. "Tasting an Imagined Thailand: Authenticity and
Culinary Tourism in Thai Restaurants." *Culinary Tourism*. Ed. Lucy
M. Long. Lexington, KY: The University Press of Kentucky,
2004. 53-75.

Nelson, William H. *The Buried Treasure: A Rabbit Hash Mystery*. Mt. Vernon,
IN: Windmill Publications, Inc., 1997.

Neustadt, Kathy. *Clambake: A History and Celebration of an American
Tradition*. Amherst: The University of Massachusetts Press, 1992.

Paredes, Americo, and Richard Bauman, eds. 1972. *Toward New Perspectives
in Folklore*. Bloomington: Trickster Press, 2000.

Pendergrast, Mark. *For God, Country and Coca-Cola: The Definitive History of
the Great American Soft Drink and the Company that Makes It*. 1993.
New York: Basic Books, 2000.

Prest, Jude. E-mail interview. January 16, 2007.

Price, Angeline F. "Working Class Whites." *Signs of Life in the USA:
Readings on Popular Culture for Writers*. Eds. Sonia Maasik and Jack
Solomon. 5th ed. Boston: Bedford/St. Martin's, 2006. 591-596.

Rabbit Hash General Store Website. February 28, 2011
<http://www.rabbithash.com/>.

Rabbit Hash Historical Society Website. March 1, 2011
<http://www.rabbithashusa.com/>.

Rabbit Hash: The Center of the Universe. Dir. Jude Prest. Sigma Home
Entertainment, 2004.

Rennick, Robert M. *From Red Hot to Monkey's Eyebrow: Unusual Kentucky
Place Names*. Lexington, KY: University Press of Kentucky, 1997.

Roberts, Warren E. *Log Buildings of Southern Indiana*. Bloomington, IN:
Trickster Press, 1996.

Santino, Jack. *All Around the Year: Holidays and Celebrations in American Life*.
Chicago: University of Illinois Press, 1994.

Schoemaker, George H. "Introcudtion: Basic Concepts of Folkloristics."
     The Emergence of Folklore in Everyday Life: A Fieldguide and Sourcebook.
     Ed. George H. Schoemaker. Bloomington, IN: Trickster Press,
     1990. 1-10.

Shartar, Martin and Norman Shavin. *The Wonderful World of Coca-Cola.*
     Atlanta: Capricorn Corporation, Inc., 1981.

Stephens, Carleen. Personal interview. November 24, 2006.

Thomas, Marlo. Personal interview. November 26, 2006.

Tommy. Personal interview. November 26, 2006.

Tuleja, Tad. "Introduction: Making Ourselves Up: On the manipulation
     of Tradition in Small Groups." *Usable Pasts: Traditions and Group
     Expressions in North America.* Ed. Tad Tuleja. Logan, UT: Utah
     State University Press, 1997. 1-20.

Turner, Rory and Phillip H. McArthur. "Cultural Performances: Public
     Display Events and Festival." *The Emergence of Folklore in Everyday
     Life: A Fieldguide and Sourcebook.* Ed. George H. Schoemaker.
     Bloomington, IN: Trickster Press, 1990. 83-93.

Turner, Victor. *The Anthropology of Performance.* New York: PAJ
     Publications, 1987.

Weslager, C.A. *The Log Cabin in America: From Pioneer Days to the Present.*
     New Brunswick, NJ: Rutgers University Press, 1969.

Yealey, A.M. *History of Boone County, Kentucky: Reprint of Articles Published in
     Newspapers Over a Period of Fifty Years.* Covington, KY: c1960.

www.ingramcontent.com/pod-product-compliance
Lightning Source LLC
Chambersburg PA
CBHW030528020726
47494CB00004B/1263